Out of the Ashes

Out of the Ashes

Book II:
The Survival Series

Travis Wright

"A free people ought not only to be armed and disciplined, but they should have sufficient arms and ammunition to maintain a status of independence from any who might attempt to abuse them, which would include their own government."

George Washington

Prologue

They pulled over on a bypass road. A few men stayed in the turrets of the Hummers just in case, but they could see for a long way up and down the road and felt safe enough to let everyone out. As the Switchblade was prepped for its flight, everyone walked around. Finally, the anticipation was over.

"We're ready to launch," Jake said.

With Joe manning the monitor, Jake launched the UAV. It gained altitude and they guided it toward the city.

It flew over the power plant first. "Guys, am I seeing people down there?" Joe asked.

A few of the others crowded around the small monitor.

"They look like they are working down there," said Steve.

"Circle around again," said James. Jake made another pass and saw they were right. "Head toward the city now," said Craig. Jake flew the Switchblade over downtown Lewiston and saw people everywhere.

"This can't be," said James. "The city is surrounded by vegetation, there are no radiation signatures above normal, and there are people all over the place. How could this be possible?" Jake continued to fly the UAV over the rest of the city and they saw even more people walking around, but no moving vehicles.

The group talked about what to do with the information they had. Jake landed the UAV and joined the conversation.

"We should be very careful here," said Craig. "With so many people we could be overrun if they want all of this." He pointed toward the vehicles.

"I agree," said Steve. "We should send a scout vehicle."

Craig, Nate, Steve and James were the best choices to go and find out if it was safe, while the rest would stay back to protect the convoy. As the scout Hummer got almost parallel across the river from the power plant, the men could see a huge road block.

They stopped. "What should we do?" James asked.

Craig looked through his binoculars. "I see dozens of armed men out there on the wall," he said. They decided that the worst thing that could happen would be the men wouldn't let them in, but then they could just open fire on them too. Nate pointed the .50 cal. to the rear. Steve got out and put a white t-shirt on the communications antenna and they drove slowly toward the heavily armed road block.

Chapter One: Apprehension

The closer the Hummer got to the huge road block, the more men formed on top and pointed their rifles at it. Steve had Craig stop about twenty feet away.

"I want to try something before we get out," he said.

Steve grabbed the head light knob and flashed in Morse code, "We come in peace and want to hurt no one." Steve repeated the message three times, got no response from the men pointing their guns at them and said, "I guess we go with plan B."

"What's plan B?" asked Craig.

"I'm making it up now," said Steve.

He took his weapons off his vest, and just as he was getting out of the Hummer, a man started to walk toward the vehicles. Steve got out and walked up to him slowly, with no weapons and his hands up. They stopped halfway between the Hummers and the road block. The two men talked for a few minutes and shook hands. Steve then walked back to the Hummer and got back in.

"What just happened?" asked James.

Craig followed with, "Yeah, what was that all about? Did you two know each other?"

"Adam recognized the Morse code from when he had been in the Navy. He came out to talk and tell me that they had a problem with nomads terrorizing the city, until they built the barriers on all the highways and in as many places as possible where they had been getting in."

"Adam huh?" asked Craig. "Are you two going to hold hands now? So can we enter or not?"

"I told him we had women and children and had come from a great distance seeking refuge. I also told him that everything else would be explained once we were inside. Adam said that they were just getting the power back on for the city, allowing them to build more barriers and get life back on track. To answer your question, yes we can enter," said Steve.

They turned the Hummer around and went back to the convoy.

The convoy was where they'd left it, and the kids were running around the vehicles. The scout Hummer pulled up and the men got out. Everyone walked quickly up to them to get the news. They knew from past group talks to let Steve or anyone else talk and then ask questions.

"The road is blocked up ahead with barbed wire all over the place, but the guards have agreed to let us through if we hand over our weapons." There were many questions at that point. "Hold on, I told Adam, the man I talked to, that we were not the people they needed to fear." Steve looked at Craig, who shrugged his shoulders. "I told him that we had families and we could help them with some of our resources. He said it had been a year since any motor vehicle had come into town. He had many questions and I told him we had answers."

"You promised him our stuff?" asked Craig.

"I said we had resources, but not what kind. They obviously know we have valuable things," said Steve, "we're driving Hummers and trucks."

The group decided to risk it and got into their vehicles.

"I want all machine guns to be pointed up as we get close to the barriers, and keep your hands off of them. We're not hostile and I want them to know that we don't want to hurt them," said Steve.

The lead Hummer pulled up to the barrier and a huge concrete block was moved out of the way. As they drove through, James was amazed with the elaborate pulley system they had set up.

"It's like a medieval crane," he said over the radio.

After the last Hummer was through and the block was lowered back into place, a group of men stopped them. Everyone was asked to get out of the trucks. Dozens of men with guns walked up to the convoy and started to introduce themselves and ask questions, about where they came from, how the trucks were running, and where they got the machine guns.

"Quiet down," said an older man as he walked over slowly with his cain holding him up and his long gray hair blowing in the slight breeze. "Who's your leader?" Steve, James and Craig all walked up to him.

"Three leaders?" asked the man. "I need to know what you plan to do here in Babylon."

"Baba-what?" asked Craig.

"Babylon," said Steve.

"Basically, the land of confusion," said James.

"Well I guess we are home then," said Craig sarcastically. "Correct me if I'm wrong, but didn't the sign a few miles back say, 'Welcome to Lewiston?'"

"We haven't changed that one yet," said a huge man with a thick German accent, as he walked up to Craig and stared him down.

"You better back off little man before you get hurt!" said Craig.

The two men just stared at each other for a few seconds, but it felt longer. Everyone on both sides stopped what they were doing, backed away and watched carefully.

"How are you Colonel?" asked the big man as he picked Craig up and hugged him. The tension quickly dissipated around the men as the six foot four, two hundred sixty pound man set Craig down.

"Slim, I never thought I would see you again," said Craig.

"You know this man Hans?" asked the old man.

"I served under him in the Marines, and I will vouch for him and his friends if you'll take it."

"I will," said the old man.

"I'm Cliff and you are all welcome here. I do want to hear where you came from and how you have all of these things."

"All in good time," said Craig.

Everyone loaded back up and the convoy drove toward the city. People poured out of buildings and houses as the small convoy drove by.

"Look at all of these people," said Joe over the radio. "How did they survive all this time after the bombs?"

"I'm sure we'll be talking for quite awhile with these people, and they'll have a lot of questions for us too," said James.

Craig's friend Hans directed them as they drove through the streets to the center of town.

The valley had been left untouched by the destructions that the rest of the world had seen. As the convoy rolled into town, the people of Lewiston couldn't believe their eyes.

The vehicles stopped outside of the county courthouse, where Craig got out and in his loud Marine Corps voice bellowed, "Who is in charge here?"

A tall skinny man with dirty clothes walked up and in a weak voice asked, "Are you the military?"

"We're not here to help you if that's what you mean," said Craig.

The old man backed away. Another man who looked well fed and clothed came out of the nearest door in the building and walked up to Craig and said, "Hello!" in a cheerful voice. "I'm the mayor and we welcome you to our wonderful city. What branch of the military are you with?" asked the man.

"Once again, we are not with the military and we are not here to save you," said Craig.

"Then why are you here?" asked the mayor.

"We came here to start over," said Steve as he got out of the lead Hummer. Many people looked confused.

"Then who are you?" the mayor asked

"We came here from Montana," said James as he approached.

"I thought Montana was destroyed two years ago," said another man.

"It was," said Steve. "We've been living underground." More people gathered. "Is there a place that we can talk?" Steve asked the mayor.

"Yes, follow me," he said.

"Wait," said Craig. "Are our vehicles and friends going to be safe out here?"

"Yes, they will," assured the mayor. "We only have to worry about Sodom and Gomorrah across the river." They all looked at him strangely. "I will explain it all, please follow me."

The three men followed the mayor into the courthouse while the rest of the group stayed outside. The occupants of the city were very intrigued and asked the waiting convoy many questions. Steve, James and Craig followed the mayor into a large meeting room and were asked to sit.

"So, you came from Montana? I'm sorry, where are my manners? My name is Daniel. Please tell me everything," he said as he parted his long black hair from his glasses.

Steve started at the beginning, with the idea of building the bunkers, and continued on with their story from the time they went underground.

"We had three bunkers and forty-two people at the beginning," said Steve "These people with us now are all that is left. We had issues with marauders that wanted in and wanted our things. We of course fought back and moved on to this place."

"Just out of curiosity," asked Daniel, "but did you hear that this was a safe haven or did you stumble upon us accidently?"

"I had a real good feeling about heading this way," said Steve.

"I know it sounds strange," said James, "but it's true. We all wanted to head toward Arizona, New Mexico or Texas, but Steve said this was the better way to go."

"Please tell us about the last two years here," asked Steve.

"We didn't get bombed of course," said Daniel, "but we did get hit with an electromagnetic pulse, from what some of our men told us. All the electronics just stopped working all of a sudden."

"I'm curious," said Steve, "how was this area not affected by the radiation from all the bombs?"

"You said you weren't bombed, and then an EMP went off later?" asked James.

"This is a valley with very tall mountains on both sides," said Daniel. "I suppose the winds and weather just worked in our favor here." When the radios went silent and the chaos started, one night there was a blinding flash that lit up the sky like it was daytime for a few minutes, and then an earthquake hit."

"The EMP," said James. "Maybe it was another strike or a delayed explosion."

8

"The lights went out and all the cars and electronics stopped working," Daniel said. "The fires and riots followed soon after."

"When the lights went out, we lost most of our local law enforcement, almost overnight. They didn't last very long with so many people to try to control in the chaos. Many people died, either from the first winter, lack of food or from the rioters. Supplies quickly diminished and we had no way to replenish anything. When people finally started to band together and share what remaining resources they had, we had lost an estimated one third of our initial population."

"Sorry to interrupt," said James, "but did anyone here die from radiation sickness?"

"None that we know of," said Daniel. "We had to deal with roving bands of dangerous people. After it started we established a new security force. That's the reason for the road blocks. We plan to encompass the entire city with a massive wall eventually. Without machinery, it has been very difficult. When we thought we had everything under control, we had people from Clarkston coming across the bridges and attacking people on this side. Until that started, we were working with them to accomplish mutual goals. We built barriers at the bridges over the Snake River and posted security all along it. Right now, we have a very unstable truce with them."

"Why is it so unstable?" asked James.

"We have the power plant that they need on our side," Daniel said, "and they keep insisting that we have had it running for months and won't share with them. We just got it running intermittently and keep having issues because of the lack of proper materials. They're getting desperate with food supplies, they're almost gone over there too."

"What do you mean almost gone?" asked Steve. "How do they have food supplies still after two years?"

"Are they growing food?" asked James.

"No, that side of the river had less people than we did," said Daniel, "and they had the food warehouse too. They horded the food and have blown through the supply. They won't listen to reason, and I'm afraid it's just a matter of time before they head our way again."

"We might be able to help you with that, and some of your other issues too," said James, "if you will take our help."

"We welcome it," said Daniel.

The men discussed plans for the power plant, the food supplies in the city and the threat outside the walls, which still needed to be finished. Much of the warehouse facilities and manufacturing plants were on the other side of the river, to the north or west now according to the compass, and had to be protected in order to accomplish their goals. With Craig knowing the big German that had served with him in the Marines, things would be much easier. If it wasn't for the two of them knowing each other, the group might not be in the city or already talking with the leadership, if at all. The mayor had been intrigued with the story of going underground and surviving the bombs and the attacks afterward. What each side had to offer helped their truce as well. The men talked for hours about everything there was to do and got well acquainted. Daniel asked them to stay for their evening meal, even though he didn't have much to offer. Steve asked Bill to have some food put together and to have Nancy and Karen come in to help with the meal for all of them. Daniel assured them that the vehicles would be safe outside while they ate.

Chapter Two: Starting Over

The city leaders offered a small warehouse to the new inhabitants from the new North. They could store the tractors, trailers and Hummers in it and still have plenty of room for living space. The warehouse used to store furniture for a nearby outlet store. Much of the merchandise was still in it and the mayor offered those to use as well. The owner had died in one of the mass riots. The space could easily be converted to house the group. The children had plenty of space to explore and run around. They were not to go outside unless they were with an adult from their main group. Safety was still a huge concern and would continue to be even after the walls surrounded the city.

Steve and James would get together with the other engineers, machinist and construction planners on the barrier projects. The electricity issue was being dealt with already and good knowledgeable men were working on it. Craig was to get together with Hans, the big German, along with Jake and Joe, to tighten the defenses and properly train and equip the members of the local security force that Hans had assembled. Hans had done a good job, but the men would now be fine tuned by the Colonel. The security force would put the Hummers into action for use if the need arose. Once the city's electricity was turned on for good, roving patrols could be assembled. There would be plenty of fuel available for them to operate. The gas station pumps didn't work at this point and with no vehicles running, it was of no concern until now. The city had abundant good, clean water and as soon as the electricity was on full time, the comforts of a civilized world would be available to everyone once again.

Nancy and some of the other women were introduced to the people that had started greenhouses dedicated to a food supply. They had had a difficult time growing produce over the last two years and hadn't grown nearly enough to feed the population. With the seeds that had been stored in the bunkers, they would have a good start, but Steve had made sure that the women didn't let them know how much they really had. With electricity, they could have year round crops of many different types. They still needed meat and dairy products. Once the bombs fell, the city ran out of food supplies rather quickly and people resorted to killing all livestock and wild game in the surrounding area in order to survive. At the time no one wanted to hear that if all the animals were killed, then there would be none left to reproduce and continue the supply. There were just too many people to feed, and this was one of the main reasons for the riots. At that point, the city's population was thinned out. Survival of the fittest was the law of the land.

Simon, one of the men from Sanctuary Two, had been a scientist and thought it was a good idea to bring a lot of his equipment out to the bunker before the bombs fell. He had also brought with him frozen embryos of many different animals, ones that had not been subject to decades of growth hormones. The idea was that once the group found or rebuilt a safe enough place, he would start growing them so they could have healthy, non-mutated farm animals to eat. The equipment and frozen embryos were still in Sanctuary Three on the other side of Hell. No one had brought up to the mayor or anyone else the fact that they had more supplies in the Billings area. A trip would have to be made to go and get the rest, but the group would wait and make sure that life in the city of New Babylon was a good one before making the trip.

Once the power plant was finally fixed to a point that it stopped fluctuating and shutting down, manufacturing of vital components to repair equipment and vehicles could resume on a regular basis. The walls surrounding the city were one of the main priorities. Cranes and heavy equipment had to be fixed for this to happen.

The days passed quickly and turned into weeks. The people of the community had accepted the new comers from Montana and everyone got along great. Everyday life wasn't much different than it had been just a couple of years before.

Once the power was back on full time, the people from across the river eventually wanted to talk. A representative was sent over to talk to the mayor.

He walked over the only bridge left across the Snake River. It was Craig's idea to destroy the other one.

"One will be easier to defend," he said. The man was met in the middle by a small security contingent. He was searched for weapons and escorted to see the mayor and the council. He was an attorney, or at least he used to be. He wore a suit and tie that had seen better days.

The man was brought to the courthouse and escorted inside.

"I'm William Sanderson," the man said as the mayor approached him.

"I'm Mayor Daniel Hunter. It's nice to meet you." The two men shook hands. "Shall we?" the mayor asked. The men walked into a meeting room where the city council was waiting.

"Please sit," said one of the councilmen.

"I won't be here long enough to sit," Sanderson said.

"What do you mean?" asked the mayor, confused.

"I have been sent here to demand your surrender," said Sanderson.

"Excuse me?" Daniel asked.

"What?" asked another from the council.

The room was full of questions. Security members moved in with their weapons drawn and pointed them at Sanderson.

"This is really unnecessary. I am just the messenger and you're not supposed to shoot the messenger, am I right?" asked Sanderson. "Oh and by the way, if I'm not back by 3 p.m. an attack will commence."

The time was 2:32 p.m. according to the clock on the wall.

"Take him to a cell," said Hans to some of the security personnel.

"You will regret your decision," said Sanderson as they put flexi cuffs on him and took him away.

"Jim, please go and get Craig and the reaction teams. Have them assemble all capable men in the warehouse nearest the bridge and tell them to be combat ready," said Hans. "Have him bring the Hummers and men in from the rear entrance so they can't be seen."

Hans and his team left to meet up with the rest of the men. Within minutes, all the security force that could be found and armed was assembled in the warehouse. Runners were sent out to all of the roadblocks as well in order to warn them of possible attack. Craig, Hans and a few others came up with a strategy to defend the city against an all out attack. Snipers would be positioned with spotters in defilade positions. Two Hummers with machine guns would be held back in support and Craig would fly the UAV around the city and coordinate the resistance with radios.

The men at the road blocks were reinforced with as many more men as could be spared from the river-front. With only one bridge to defend, not as many men would be needed there, they hoped. The rest of the river-bank had been lined with barbed wire just in case anyone decided to swim over and try to climb the bank.

Craig launched the Switchblade just before three and started to tell the rest what he was seeing.

"There are a lot of men massing on the river-side," said Craig over the radio. "I see a large group moving to the east to flank us."

At exactly 3 p.m. the river-front exploded with rifle and machine-gun fire.

"Let them waste their ammo," said Joe over the radio.

Joe, Jake and a few other snipers shot targets of opportunity. They would shoot a few men firing in their direction then displace to a new position. By firing from inside of a room in the buildings, the snipers would be harder to detect from the outside. The fire from across the river lasted just a few minutes and then a large group amassed and started to run across the bridge. One Hummer was called in to engage them. The people reached the barricade in the center of the bridge and as they crossed it were torn to pieces by the .50 cal. on top the Hummer. Fire from the other side started up again and hit the armor on the vehicle, but it was well protected and nothing got through. Craig directed another Hummer to a different part of the city as he saw a large group moving into position.

Craig couldn't keep the UAV up continuously, but as he heard sporadic fire through the night, he would launch it to keep an eye on things as best he could.

"Not much of an attack," Hans said to Craig as he walked up on the roof in the morning. "The way the man was talking, it sounded like it would be a war."

"Did we lose anyone?" asked Craig.

"A few of the men on the perimeter below that wanted to see what was happening and wouldn't keep their heads down," he said. "Natural selection if you ask me."

"Has anyone questioned the man that came to demand our surrender?" asked Craig.

"Not yet, we've been a little busy," said Hans.

"Would you like me to go and work my magic with him?" asked Craig, smiling.

"Be my guest. When can I launch this baby again?" asked Hans.

"In about twenty minutes," said Craig.

The courthouse is a couple of blocks away, that'll be a nice morning walk, thought Craig. He was walking by the warehouse the others were staying in when Kyle walked out.

"How is it out there?" he asked Craig.

"Not much happening right now, how's the wound?"

"Gary said it's healing nicely and I can rejoin the ranks soon. Are you hungry? We just started breakfast."

"Thanks, but I have an interrogation to attend to. I'll stop by later and see if there's any left," said Craig.

"I'll save you some," Kyle said.

Craig thanked him and walked on to the courthouse. There were a couple of men standing guard by the front.

"We heard the gunfire through the night," said one of them.

"How does it look out there?" asked the other man.

"I'm going to find out right now," said Craig as he walked by them and entered the building. Craig walked into the basement and to the cells where he found the mayor talking with Sanderson over breakfast.

"Excuse me," said Craig, "but why is he eating a gourmet meal while men are defending this city with nothing hot to eat or drink?" Craig moved toward them and a large man stepped in front of him.

"I'm trying to reach an agreement here," said the mayor in a condescending tone.

"What do they want?" asked Craig.

"We just want to join you and the rest of society over here," said Sanderson as he took another bite of his breakfast.

"Mayor, we can defend this city and everyone in it," said Craig. "We have heard and you know what kind of people are over there, and they have no place in this city."

"This is a new world," said Sanderson, "and we just want to live in peace."

"I have a hard time believing that," said Craig. He turned around and walked out.

Craig called for a meeting of the group from the bunker over the radio. Everyone was to meet back at the warehouse they had been living in.

Steve met him at the front of the warehouse. "How did the interrogation go?" he asked.

"There wasn't one. The mayor was having breakfast with the man from the other side like they were old friends."

"Let's go eat and we can talk when everyone else gets here," said Steve.

After the rest of the group got back and ate they had a meeting with Craig up front.

"I know it's usually Steve up here," he said, "but I've been thinking about what is best for this group and staying here in the city is not it. With the mayor working with the undesirables from across the river, it won't be safe here long term. I've scouted out an area just south west of here. It's an old airstrip with a few hangars," said Craig. "We can build a nice living area and watch the entire perimeter from the old control tower. It's a good option for us and we can secure it pretty easily. We will need to clear out a few left-over aircraft, but it has great vantage points."

"Does anyone have questions?" asked Craig.

"What will we tell the mayor and his people?" asked James. "We said we would help out here."

"We need to think about our own safety," said Steve. "This group is what's important. If they want to invite undesirables in here to live with, that's on them. We'll go and look at the area with Craig and make a decision as a group. We will then talk to the mayor about either decision we make. We also need to get back to the bunkers and get the rest of the gear, equipment, tools and food soon."

"I agree," said Craig. "Either way this goes down, we need the rest of our stuff."

A cease fire had been called and the mayor let Sanderson go. Not everyone in the city was happy about that and there was talk all over about leaving. This was the group's way out of the situation. They all went out to the airstrip and saw the potential that Craig had seen.

The mayor understood the reason they wanted to move outside the city and didn't try to talk them out of it. He didn't like the fact that Hans and a few other men were going with them.

"We need you here," he told Hans.

"I have trained these men and I make my own decisions. It appears you'll have all the men you will need when they cross the river. Thank you for taking me in when I needed your help." With that, Hans left to help his friends build the new perimeter they needed to keep all of them safe.

Two days after they moved out to the remote airstrip, Craig said that they should go back to get their stuff. Jake would stay to oversee construction while Craig, Steve, Kyle, Ray, Nate and Hans would go down the road back to the Billings area. Two Hummers and one tractor with a trailer would go. They hoped they would have enough room to bring everything back. On the way there, they would have someone on both Hummer gun turrets. On the way back, someone would have to drive the tanker truck, leaving them more vulnerable.

Chapter Three: Road Trip

Karen didn't want Steve to leave, but he reassured her that they would be back in a few days.

"The road should still be the way we left it unless someone built another road block by Bozeman," he told her.

Jake and the rest of the men set off the next morning to work on the perimeter. Steve and the others got in the vehicles and drove away. With any luck, they would be able to drive straight through in one day and return in two more days. They planned on spending one night back in the bunker so they weren't on the road at night. When the small convoy reached the outskirts of the city and the road block, the guards opened it right up to let them through.

Jake had drawn up a detailed version of the airstrip and the surrounding area after seeing a bird's eye view from the UAV monitor. An old chain link fence covered almost the entire perimeter and would act as a first line of defense after the trip wires with flares were positioned just beyond it with claymores and land mines in between the two. A minefield would be put in place in the area with no fence. Mixtures of anti-personnel and anti-vehicle mines were to be put into the ground. A trench would be dug on the airstrip side for personnel to shoot from once the bobcat was brought back from the bunker to dig it.

As the women were setting up sleeping areas in the main hanger, the kids discovered a full basement while they played. Karen decided that it would be converted for the new housing area as soon as possible.

"When the rest of the men return, we will make this our new home," she said to the others.

The other women agreed that it would be safer and warmer in the winter too.

"Joe, how do things look up there?" asked Steve.

"The road is still clear," said Joe, who had driven up ahead in one of the Hummers to make sure the tractor and trailer could get through.

"We're making real good time," said Nate.

It would take more than eight hours, but as long as the road was still clear they would make it back to the bunker by nightfall.

The children were asked to help, but soon found themselves exploring the new area instead.

"We need to go back and help," said Olivia to the others.

"I want to see what's in this building," said Billy.

"I'm going to tell," Allie said.

"Why do you have to ruin things?" asked Carl. "We just wanna have fun."

"We're supposed to be helping and it would all get done faster if we did," said Olivia. "See, someone is calling for us. Let's go, all of you."

The kids all walked back to the hangar, where Kim questioned them. "Where have you all been? I've been looking for you. We need to get everything set up in here and need your help. You kids will be living here too."

"I'm sorry Kim," said Olivia, "but they wouldn't listen to me."

"You kids need to listen to Olivia and all of the adults," said Kim. "We're here to protect you. It's a different world we live in, a harder and more violent one. There will be plenty of time for exploring once we have set up living, cooking, school and entertainment areas," said Kim. "I need you all to go down to the basement and help organize it please."

The kids did as they were told and started walking down the stairs very slowly.

"Craig, this is Joe, over."

"Go ahead buddy," said Craig.

"We need to launch the UAV up ahead and scout the area."

"Roger that," said Craig.

The convoy stopped and everyone got out to find out why Joe had stopped them.

They had made it past Missoula and were heading toward Butte when Joe saw something on the road down the mountain.

Craig launched the Switchblade and Steve manned the monitor.

As the UAV climbed, the scene on the road became clear.

"I see a lot of people on the road," said Steve, "and they're headed this way."

"How many?" asked Hans.

"Too many to fight off," said Craig. "I'm turning this thing around and looking for an alternate route for us to take."

On the way back to the convoy with the UAV, Craig noticed a farm house out of the way and told the others, "That's where we need to go."

Everyone got in the vehicles and went down the road toward the farm. There was a barn by the house. Joe got out of his Hummer and opened the door. He went inside to make sure it was clear and backed Nate in so the tractor and trailer was out of sight.

The two Hummers would be positioned beside the house and the barn to have overlapping fire if needed. Craig launched the UAV again to monitor the situation. "They're now passing the driveway," Craig said after about twenty minutes.

"I estimate there are hundreds of them," said Steve. "Wait, a few of them are coming this way."

"Lock and load," said Craig as he brought the UAV back to earth.

There were five men and women that had left the group, most likely to see if there was anything worth salvaging down at the end of the drive.

The rest of the people walking were hundreds of yards down the highway by the time the five people reached the house. They entered the house and the convoy rolled out of the area. The plan to avoid the people had worked.

"We're over an hour behind schedule now," said Steve, "but we should still make it there before nightfall as long as nothing else happens."

The convoy continued as fast as they could. Meanwhile, they all wondered where the people had come from and where they were headed.

The men working on the perimeter had taken MRE's out for lunch, but wanted a hot meal for dinner. They made a big dent in securing the new area in the first day and would continue early the next morning. The mines and trip wires were drawn on the map in order to keep track of them.

When they got back, the women and children were nowhere to be found. Jake didn't like this and issued an order for pairs of men to search different areas.

"I want you to check in every five minutes until they're found," he said.

Awhile later, Bill told everyone on the radio that he had located all of the women and children in the back of the main hangar.

The men all converged on the area to find out what was going on.

"They found a full basement under this hangar," said James.

"Did any of you guys know that was down there?" asked Jake of the men from the city.

"I'm not even from around here," said one man.

"I've lived here for years and I have never been out here," said another.

"Well, I think you ladies have found our new home," said Jake. "We can build a false room right here where the stairs go down and no one will know where we are. How does it look down below?"

"It can be retrofitted in no time," said Karen. "We'll need lights installed in many areas, but it will be nice to live in."

"Once it's done, it'll look just like the bunkers," said Nancy.

"You guys must be starving," said Kim. "Ladies let's get these hungry men fed."

The sun had gone down and temporary lighting was put in place. Most everyone would sleep in tents since there was not enough room in the trailer. A watch was figured out amongst the men. Kim and Nancy volunteered to stand watch also.

"We know you men are going to be working hard and long in the sun all day," said Nancy. "We will stand watch as well."

"I will stand watch also," said Theresa.

"Well," said Jake, "it looks like we have plenty of people to cover the whole night. Sven and Logan, if you want to sleep in the same tent and get a good night's sleep we can cover watch tonight. Hopefully we will get close to finishing the security tomorrow and we won't need to have as many people stay up all night again."

Jake made a roster and Bill smiled when he saw he would be standing watch with Theresa for two hours. Theresa saw him smiling, but didn't say anything.

The small convoy reached what was left of Billings just after dark. It had taken the men thirteen hours to make it back to their old home. They rolled up on the compound they had built and made their way through the minefield using night vision. They had marked the mines with infrared paint so they could find their way through without setting any off. Craig and Steve opened the gate and walked toward Sanctuary Three. The others stayed back and looked out for any trouble.

"It doesn't look like anyone has disturbed anything," said Steve on the radio for everyone to hear.

"We're going to open the bunker up," said Craig.

The two men opened the hatches and went inside. Within minutes, the outside lights came on and the convoy moved into the compound.

"We'll work until midnight," said Craig. "You know what to do, so get it done."

The men split up into teams and loaded the vehicles with all that they could. If it looked like they would have to make another trip, the battery banks and infrastructure of the Sanctuary would stay intact; otherwise they would gut everything and leave it for anyone else to have. They had left the bunker running on minimal power to keep the refrigeration and heating systems going.

At 2 a.m. Bill was woken up to stand watch. Theresa was soon beside him in the tower.

"How have you been?" she asked him.

"I'm doing good, thank you for asking."

Bill continued to look through the night vision and handed the thermal imaging monocular to Theresa.

"Thank you," she said.

"Have you been avoiding me, or have we just been that busy?" asked Theresa.

"Why would you ask me that?" said Bill.

"I just want to make sure I haven't done anything to upset you," she said.

"Now what could you possibly do to upset me?" asked Bill. "I've kept my distance from you because I don't trust myself."

"What do you mean Bill?" Theresa asked as she grabbed his hand.

The two looked at each other and slowly moved closer for a kiss. They kissed passionately for a few minutes and then Bill pulled her in front of him and held her.

"I've wanted to do that for some time," he told her. "I know now that what I've been feeling is real, and not a longing for my wife."

Theresa held on to him tighter and continued to look at the perimeter. She knew what he meant and was glad for what they had.

The next morning, the men at Sanctuary Three woke up early to finish the packing.

"Do you think we will need to come back for any of the stuff we can't fit in this time?" Steve asked Craig.

"We'll secure it all and if we need it, we know where to find it," said Craig.

Not everything fit into the vehicles. The rear Hummer would tow a trailer with the bobcat on it. Some machinery and building materials could not be brought this time, but the rest of the food, clothing, weapons and ammo were loaded up. The trailer had four-wheelers and motorcycles crammed into it as well. The men were exhausted and not looking forward to the return trip, but it had to be done. They would get back after dark, and didn't like the fact that they would be driving in that late without more support.

"Should we stay one more night?" asked Ray. "We could get more sleep and leave here at first light."

"We told the rest of the group that we would be back in two to three days," said Craig, "and that's what we will do. We can try to contact them on the radio when we get closer to get some relief out; otherwise it's up to us."

The convoy drove out of the compound and locked the gates. They were on their way back with much needed gear and supplies.

"I hope the guys get everything we need to turn the basement into a living area," said Kim.

"I think we will have everything we need, and the man power to do it," said Nancy.

The women continued to work on the basement to get it ready and to keep their minds off their men and the convoy. The security detail that was left behind to work on the perimeter continued to put out trip wires and mines.

James was busy putting up a communications array on the old control tower. He wanted to be able to stay in contact with the group, find other survivors and find out what really happened to the world. He had finished by mid afternoon and started putting the windmill up. He would need help to finish it, but they still had enough juice in the battery banks to last a few more days with minor consumption. The old airstrip had power out to it at one time, but too many electrical poles were down and the line had been separated from the grid. They told the mayor that they would be fine without the city's power.

The men putting up the perimeter called it quits again just after the sun went down. They got back just as Kim was getting ready to go and get them.

"Dinner smells great ladies," said Logan, one of the men that had joined them.

"Thank you," said a few of the women together.

"Any word yet on the convoy?" Jake asked James.

"Nothing yet I'm afraid. I'm going to try to reach them again as soon as I'm done eating."

"I'll join you," said Jake.

The men enjoyed the meal and then walked over to the small communication room that James had put together.

"Convoy, this is home base, can you read me?" said James over the radio.

James tried it a few more times and got nothing. The men were starting to walk away from the equipment when they heard a faint and garbled voice.

"Can you boost the signal?" asked Jake.

"I can't until we get more power," said James. "They will have to get closer for us to hear them." James gave the person on the other end instructions to try to contact them every five minutes. In about twenty minutes, they could hear almost clearly.

"This is Craig in the convoy, can you hear me?"

"Craig, this is James, I can hear you now."

"We could hear you when you first started to transmit," said Craig but I guess you couldn't hear me.

"Your signal must have been too weak," said James. "Where are you guys?"

"We are passing Kamiah and should be there soon. Can you send a Hummer to the main gate and let them know that we're friendly?"

"I'm on my way," said James.

Everyone was excited about the news of the convoy. James took Logan and Bill with him to the road block. The last thing they needed was someone firing on the convoy as it approached.

The men reached the road block in record time and got out to talk to the men standing guard.

"Our friends will be coming up to the blockade very soon," said James. "They should have four vehicles this time."

"Good to know," said a man that approached them. "Did they get what they went out for?"

"We don't know yet," said Bill, "but we hope they did."

Sometime later in the evening, a man on top said, "There are trucks approaching."

James got on the radio. "Craig, this is James, where are you?"

"We have the road block in sight," said Craig.

"They are friendlies," said the man on the ground to everyone else.

The huge block of concrete was moved out of the way and the convoy drove through. They stopped on the other side and thanked the men on guard duty. They also told them about the large group of people they had seen migrating down the highway.

"Let's get home," said Steve, and everyone agreed.

The convoy rolled through the gate in front of the airstrip to a huge reunion. The men had only been gone for two days, but it seemed like weeks had gone by.

"You stink," Karen said to Steve. "But I'll ignore it so you can see your son."

"I missed you," said Kim to Ray.

"I missed you too baby!"

"You guys need showers," said Nancy. "I'll go and get everything ready for you."

The men all went and took showers and ate a late meal. They were exhausted, but eager to hear about the progress that had been made on the security.

"We found a full basement right below us," said Sally. "It's been cleaned up and can be converted as a living area for all of us."

The men from the convoy were intrigued and couldn't wait to see it.

"We'll show you all of it in the morning," said Kim. "Right now I think we should get some sleep."

Jake made up a security roster and those picked for watch went to their post's as the rest of them went to bed.

Chapter Four: Remodeling

They unloaded everything that they had brought back from the bunkers on this trip and laid it out on the hangar floor so everyone could get a better idea of what they had to work with. Steve, Ray and James drew up a construction plan. The basement was lit up with construction lights brought in by two of the men that had recently joined the group. They knew where the lights were stored and had gone to get them.

Jake enlisted Joe and Craig to help finish the perimeter security. They would all aid in the construction once they were satisfied they would be safe.

"We have four main rooms down here," said James. "We can split them up for living quarters and build a main area in the middle for a kitchen and dining room."

Large concrete pillars were positioned throughout the basement.

"There is a hallway leading off of this room," said Ray.

Everyone walked over to meet him and look at the hallway.

"Ray, you and Sam go down and see where it leads," said Steve. "The rest of you, let's build some walls and rooms for everyone."

James went back up to the surface to continue work on the windmill. He would let the others know when he needed help erecting it. A few of the kids asked James if they could help him. Allie was staring at the communication tower and array that he had built on top of it. "Would you like to try to talk to people?" he asked her. Allie nodded her head yes. "Follow me," James said.

James showed Allie the communications room at the top of the tower and showed her how to use the radio and tune it in. "If you aren't sure about something, come and ask me," said James.

"I will and thank you," said Allie.

"By early afternoon, the men on the perimeter were happy with the security they had put in place. James was ready to put the windmill into action.

"Can you guys help me?" James asked the men as they walked back into the hangar.

"What do you have going on?" asked Craig.

"I'm putting the windmill together and need help to finish it and put it up," said James.

The men went out back to see what he needed. James had been busy and once they helped him stand the windmill up, they would have all the power they would need.

A few hours later, they had operational wind power and when James hooked everything into the transformer, all that they needed ran.

Ray and Sam had walked for a few hundred yards down the hallway and came to a door.

"Should we open it?" asked Sam.

"I'm not sure," said Ray. "Let's go and get the others and see what they think."

The two men walked back down the hallway and could soon see a bright light.

"They must have gotten the electricity on," said Ray, as they got closer to the main room.

The men walked into the large room and met up with the others.

"We have a door down the hallway a few hundred yards," said Ray.

"What's on the other side?" asked Steve.

"We didn't want to open it without taking some precautions," said Ray. "We should take a Geiger counter and a camera if we have it."

"Masks wouldn't be a bad idea either," said Craig as he walked up.

"How does the security look up there?" asked Steve.

"The guys did an excellent job," said Craig. "This is a nice area down here," he commented.

"We need to get ventilation down here and within a week or so, we can be living in it full time," said Steve. "Craig, can you help Ray and Sam with the door and find out what's on the other side?"

"I would be happy to," said Craig. "Let's go and get the equipment we need boys, and let's get that thing opened up."

The construction of the new living area continued and up above the women and children worked on a greenhouse that they could grow food in year around.

"We should grow some plants for the basement too," said Nancy.

"Great idea," said Karen as she worked with the baby attached to her front.

The greenhouse was being built in an upstairs room in the hangar. The room had large windows and would allow more light to come in. With the insulation of the building, it was a perfect choice for an indoor greenhouse.

"We should see about getting some skylights cut into the roof," said Nancy.

"That's a great idea," said Karen.

Luckily, they had only brought out a small portion of the seeds they actually had when they were helping the people in the city with theirs.

Kim had taken some of the kids into the woods to get moss to cover the new plants and keep the moisture in the soil so they would grow faster. Joe was escorting her and the kids along with Logan, one of the new men from the city. They were taking no chances and had full combat gear on just in case. Joe would stop every now and then and scout the area with a thermal monocular.

They gathered everything they needed in a short amount of time.

On their way back from the trip to the woods, Joe was on rear security with Logan in the front. Joe stopped to scan the area and saw that they were being followed.

"Anyone on this frequency, this is Joe. We are half a click out from the mine field and on our way back from the woods. We're being followed and need a reaction team to meet us on the perimeter ASAP."

Logan turned around as he heard the call on the radio and Joe motioned for him to keep going.

"Get your night vision out and guide us through the mine field," Joe said on the radio.

Logan kept going and saw the reaction team making their way toward them. Everyone filed through the mine field in a straight line following Logan once they got there. The group met the reaction team in the trench that had been started on the field side. The people following them stopped for some reason.

"Kim, get the kids back and let everyone know to stay inside," said Jake.

"This will cut our construction time short today," said Craig.

"It was getting close to quitting time anyway," said Steve.

"The people that were following us are leaving the area," said Joe, as he looked through the thermal monocular.

"Let's go guys," said Craig. "We can monitor the situation better from the tower, and besides, it's dinner time."

The group walked back to the hangar and started a watch rotation. They all knew that with the security they had put in place that they were safe from even a large force. They started dinner and construction on everything came to a halt for the day. James suggested that signs for the entire perimeter be made up for the mine field. Craig didn't like warning people, but what if a kid or innocent people walked into them? No one wanted to live with that, so a group was designated to make the signs the next day.

The night was uneventful and everyone was glad for it. They all knew that in a short time, the hard labor would be over and they could enjoy life.

Simon was eager to get started on growing live-stock from the frozen embryos that were brought back. With his equipment in place in a side room and steady electricity, he could start growing them. His injuries were still healing and with missing fingers, he would need help. He asked the women before they went to work if any of them would be interested in helping him with his project. Susan, Trevor's wife, agreed to help.

"I raised animals in 4H when I was growing up," she said. "I'm sure you can show me the rest."

"You'll do just fine," he told her.

The two of them went off to work on the project of growing animals. Simon had talked to Steve and James about what to do with the animals once they were born. One of the small hangars would be converted to house all the animals in order to keep them in one place. They couldn't let them roam free and definitely didn't want anyone on the outside to see them. Within a year, they would have fully matured animals that would be pro-ducing milk, mating and be ready to butcher as long as everything worked out. Nancy mentioned that she would want the manure for the greenhouse once they got to that point. It would help the crops grow faster and bigger.

Everyone had jobs to do and they were all working well together. Sherri had found a dry erase board in one of the trailers that had been used while the kids were in school mode. Now that it was summer time, she could use it to put all projects on the board and who was working on what. This came in handy. Everyone could see what was going on around the compound and how things were progressing.

"Who do you think those people were that were following us yesterday?" Joe asked Jake as they worked in the new living area.

"They could just be travelers, or people from the city wanting to know what we are up to," said Jake.

"Are you two girls just going to talk all day or actually help out?" asked Craig.

"You do realize you are talking shit to two people don't you?" asked Joe.

"I do Suzie, and if you and your girlfriend need an ass kicking, I would be more than happy to oblige."

"Can you guys take it easy over there and help out so we can get all of this done?" asked James.

"I'm just messing with the love birds," said Craig laughing.

Jake slapped Craig on the ass as he walked by and said, "Good game!"

Everyone was laughing now except for Craig. Hans was laughing the loudest.

"You just got punked Colonel!" he said.

"We have a great group of guys here," Steve said to James.

"We have a great group of people," said James.

The men kept working and the basement was slowly being transformed into what looked like the inside of a house.

With the interruption of the visitors the day before, Craig, Ray and Sam never got to see what was on the other side of the door in the hallway.

At the end of the day, Craig walked up to Ray. "Do you still want to know what is on the other side of your door?" he asked.

"I sure do," said Ray. "Sam, you want to go down the hall before dinner?"

"Sure, why not," said Sam.

The three men put their masks on and took some equipment down the hall to investigate. Craig was watching the Geiger counter and it registered normal the whole way and up to the door. The door was solid and appeared to be sealed from the inside. Craig had Sam drill a hole in the bottom of it so he could put a snake camera through it and look on the other side. When Sam was done, Craig started to push the snake through. He turned on the light and immediately saw a staircase.

"That's interesting," said Craig. "We're in a basement already and now we have stairs going down further. I'm getting no readings of any kind."

"Should we open the door now?" asked Sam.

"Let's get more guys down here and a plasma cutter," said Craig. "I want to put locks on the door with clasps before we breach. We don't know what may be down there, so I want to secure it if we need to."

The men left the hallway and went to eat dinner and discuss everything with the rest of the group.

"I agree with Craig about being cautious," said Steve. "We don't want to do anything we might regret. We can open it up and go in before we start work in the morning."

Everyone relaxed for the rest of the evening and those who had a shift on watch got ready for it.

"We will continue a lookout for a while longer," said Steve. "We have a lot to protect and can't afford to lose anyone else."

Everyone agreed and with the extra men that had joined the group, things would hopefully be easier.

Another uneventful night passed by and after breakfast the next morning, all of the men went into the basement to open the door at the end of the hallway. There weren't enough masks for all of them, so the others stayed back at the main rooms. They installed the latches and moved in the plasma cutter. Ray cut down the seam on the right side and they were able to open the door. There was a deadbolt on the top and one on the bottom and a handle on the other side. There were no harmful readings, so the men moved in and down the spiral staircase. It went down a few floors, until they reached another door just like the one on top.

"This is getting real weird," said Joe.

"What do we do now?" asked James.

"I have an idea," said Steve. He started tapping on the door in Morse code.

"We are not here to hurt you, we are friends," he said out loud as he tapped.

Steve repeated it a couple more times and then a camera popped out of the wall above the door.

"Who are you?" asked a man's voice from somewhere.

"We're from Montana," said Steve. "We mean you no harm. We're living on the surface and discovered this place. Are you living in a bunker?"

"If you really are there, then the war is over?" asked the man.

"The war only lasted a day as far as we know," said James. "We ourselves just recently emerged from our bunkers and are starting a new life on the surface. Would you like to come out and talk?"

There was silence for a while, and then the door opened.

A blinding light came from the doorway, then faded to a normal light they could handle. Three men came out pointing guns at everyone. They ordered Steve's group to drop their guns.

"I'll put mine down when you do," said Craig.

One man came forward. "This is our bunker friend and we will tell you how it will be," he said.

"We have more men at the top of the stairs and our families are in the hangar above," said Steve. "We really are the people we say we are. Please let us tell you our story, and we want to hear yours. We can take you to the top so you can see we are good, decent people."

"I tell you what," said the man who seemed to be in charge. "You leave one man here with no weapons and I will go with you to verify your story."

"That would work just fine," said Steve.

"I'll stay," said James.

With that, the men swapped places and the group returned to the surface with the man they found down below.

"I see you've been busy," commented the man as they walked by the basement.

"We've been converting the whole area into a place for us to rebuild," said Steve. "We had no idea that you were down there. I'm going to assume that you own all of this?"

"Well that was the idea, buddy, and yes I do," said the man.

Steve stopped and turned around.

"I'm so sorry," he said. "I'm Steve Miller and these are my friends Ray, Sam, Jake and Joe." The rest of the men introduced themselves.

"My name's Chris Steglich," said the tall lean man who appeared to be in his forties or fifties. "This structure, land and airstrip are mine. I know there was no way for you to know we were here or that you were trespassing. I will hear your story and make my decision about you staying here."

"I look forward to telling it to you!" said Steve excitedly.

The men all went up the stairs into the hangar and Chris's eyes got big.

"Are you part of the military?" asked Chris after seeing the Hummers and machine guns.

"We are not," said Craig, "but many of us were in the military. We're just like you and survived just like you."

Sherri walked out of a side room and looked around at all the men.

"Where's James?" she asked.

"He's down below with the new people we found," said Steve. "Sherri, this is Chris and he's from the bunker that we just found down below."

She walked over and shook his hand. "It's very nice to meet you." she said. "Is my husband ok?"

"He's fine ma'am and will not be harmed," said Chris with a smile.

A few more of the women came down from upstairs when they heard all the talking.

"Chris, this is my wife Karen and son De Novo," said Steve.

"A baby," said Chris. "How wonderful and a fitting name given our circumstances. Steve, I'm ready to hear your story."

"Take a break everyone," said Steve. "You know Latin?" he asked Chris.

"Latin and a few other languages," said Chris.

The two men started walking outside and Steve started telling his and his friends' story. They walked around the perimeter and a few hours later came back.

"I've decided to let you stay," said Chris, "but please remember that this is my place and you are all guests. We can live in harmony here as long as everyone can get along."

Chris and Steve went down below to the bunker and to get James, who was probably wondering what was going on.

"This place used to be a missile silo," said Chris. "The airstrip was built on top of it and it wasn't hard to convert to the living quarters we have now. We have more room than we know what to do with really." They reached the door at the bottom of the spiral stairway. James was sitting on the floor and stood up when he saw them.

"Well?" asked James. "Can I go home now?"

"Actually James, why don't you come down with us and see our home. I'm Chris by the way, and your guards here are David and Ben."

The men went down into the old silo-turned-bunker. Steve and James couldn't believe how big it was.

The men in the basement got off to a late start, but could still get a lot done with the rest of the day they had left. The news of the bunker below them spread out to everyone. The thought of more people was a concern for some. A bunker down below with people living in it meant more supplies. Whether or not they would share was another story.

Chapter Five: Friends Down Below

Chris led the men down three more flights of stairs and through another blast door. The first room was an entertainment area. The next level was the kitchen and storage. The next below it was the living quarters and then the last level was more storage, armory and mechanical.

"This is amazing," said Steve. "It's almost just like ours. Who built it for you?"

"Jim Reed from Clandestine Construction retrofitted it for me," said Chris.

Steve and James stared at each other.

"Did he build yours too?" asked Chris when he saw their surprised looks.

"He did actually," said James.

"Fantastic," said Chris. "Well, introductions then. This is my wife, Kerri, and our daughters Silvia and Rachel. Everyone, these are the people that live upstairs, Steve and James."

Everyone was introduced and drinks were poured. The men and women talked for hours. The story that James and Steve told was very interesting to everyone.

"We'd like to go up and meet their wives and everyone else," said Kerri after a while.

"We'll get to that," said Chris. "They're in the process of building living areas and we will let them finish. We don't want to interrupt them."

"Look at the time," said Steve as he looked at his watch. "We should get back for dinner and help the other men."

"It was very nice to meet all of you," said James as he got up slowly, not realizing how much he had drank.

They all said goodnight and the men walked back up the stairs.

Back up top, dinner was just getting done when Steve and James walked into the hangar.

"It's about time mister," Karen said to Steve. "Your son was wondering where you were. Have you been drinking?"

"They were very hospitable," hiccupped James.

There were all kinds of questions from everyone and some laughter directed ath the obviously drunk men.

"We will get to all of your questions right after James and I eat something," said Steve.

Most of the group sat around and waited for them to get done eating.

"Ok," said Steve, once he was done with his meal. "Chris has agreed to let us stay here as long as there is no trouble. We can use their help and they can use ours."

"They were as surprised as we were about other people living here," said James. "We have resources and so do they. We can all work together to get back to some sort of a normal life."

The next day, everyone went about their duties to get as much done as possible. A woman appeared in the basement while the men were working. Some of them stared and Steve went over to her.

"Good morning Kerri," said Steve, who looked a little under the weather. "Are we being too loud?"

"We can't hear you from the bunker," she said. "But I would like to meet your wife and your son if you don't mind."

"Not at all," said Steve. "Please follow me."

The two went upstairs and Steve found Karen. Kerri introduced herself and Steve left them to get acquainted.

Construction of the living area was almost finished. The air exchange unit was ready to be put in place. The vent piping would go up by the stairs and then through the roof of the hangar. They still had to build a room above the stairs to hide the basement. Steve wanted to go and talk to Chris to make sure that everything they were doing was okay. Craig wanted to see the converted missile silo, so he went with him.

"This is incredible," said Craig, as they descended into the living area.

"I have a feeling that Chris was someone important before the end of the world," said Steve.

The door at the bottom was open, but Steve knocked on the door anyway. They heard nothing, so the two men walked in and called out.

"Hello," said Steve.

"Down here," said a voice.

The men walked down the stairs and into the main area of the first level.

"Chris, this is Craig, you may remember him from last night."

"Yes I do." Chris shook his hand.

"I wanted to see if you could come topside so I can go over what we would like to do to the basement and hangar, if you have some free time," said Steve.

"I can go up and talk to you in a while," said Chris. "We're moving some gear right now and getting ready to reassemble my jet."

"Your jet?" asked Steve.

"Yes, we took it completely apart and brought it down here so nothing would happen to it. If I had left it in one of the hangars while we were down here, there's no telling what might have been done to it."

"That's very interesting," said Steve. "You'll be able to go up and actually see what the world looks like now."

"Precisely," said Chris, "and we can go wherever we want."

"Were you rich before the world ended?" asked Craig.

"Craig, why would you ask that?" asked Steve.

"It's a legitimate question," said Chris. "Yes, to answer your question. I was very wealthy Craig. I spent a large portion of the money I had on preparing for what I saw as the inevitable. We have more than you could imagine stored here and many other places. I didn't know where we would be, so I built multiple facilities like this around the country. I don't have the firepower that you have and that's one reason I've decided to team up with you, if you want to of course."

"We would be more than happy to!" said Steve excitedly.

"Then," said Chris, "you can do what you need to for your people and we will help with whatever we can."

"Thank you!" said Steve.

Craig and Steve shook hands with Chris again and went back up top.

"There's something about that guy," said Craig.

"What do you mean?" asked Steve.

"I don't know," said Craig. "Something just doesn't feel right."

"I don't have that feeling," said Steve. "Please let me know before you do anything okay?"

"You got it boss," said Craig.

"He's beautiful," said Kerri to Karen. "Did you plan to have him, or was he a surprise?"

"He was a surprise actually," said Karen. "How old are your girls?"

"Fourteen and sixteen and they're a handful," said Kerri. "They had the hardest time in the beginning when we went to live underground."

"We had a few kids like that too," said Karen. "They got used to everything though, and are going to be better people for it later on."

"I agree," said Kerri. "I'm going to get back home now and let you get back to work. I just had to see the baby. I believe the saying even more now."

Karen was about to ask her, what saying, but the other woman spoke first.

"You know, how a baby is God's way of saying that the world should go on."

"Yes," said Karen, "I believe that as well."

Kerri hugged De Novo and Karen and said, good-bye.

Karen got back to work in the greenhouse and Kerri went back down stairs. With the perimeter secure, everyone could concentrate on their assigned duties.

Steve was curious about the jet. He decided he would go and talk to Chris the following morning and try to get more information about what their plans were.

Chris and the other two men, David and Ben, were busy hauling the jet parts up to the small hangar at the front of the airstrip. The elevator that Chris had installed made moving everything so much easier. The forklift moved the pallets around with ease and reassembly wouldn't take long at all. Ben was Chris's brother in-law and David was Chris's right hand. David was an aeronautical engineer and Ben was an aircraft mechanic.

Once Chris talked with Steve and found out about the perimeter security, he knew that it was time to put the jet back together. He knew it would be safe and they could take it up with no problems.

"Do you trust these new people?" David asked Chris.

"Out of anyone in the world that could have shown up on our door step," said Chris. "I believe that these are good and honorable people. With the families that they have and the way that they protect them, I think we can learn to trust each other."

"I for one am glad that they put up a security wall around us," said Ben.

"That's the main reason we're up here doing this, brother," said Chris.

"We should have this beauty back together in a few weeks," said David.

The men planned on putting in long hours, and would thoroughly test each system they put back together. Chris had stored enough fuel for a few decades. The containers were all stored underground, kept cool and were run through pumps on a timer. This helped maintain the octane level and ensure the fuel didn't go bad.

"When do you think they will ask for supplies?" asked Ben.

"I don't know that they will," said Chris. "They are prepared for anything and have a huge arsenal of various weapons to back it up. We might need something from them before they do from us. They're building a greenhouse in the loft above the hangar and they have a scientist growing farm animals from frozen embryos. I couldn't believe that one when I heard it. I think we'll be able to help each other out."

The men continued to work on the jet and by early afternoon, their wives had come up to bring them lunch. Life was slowly getting back to normal for all of them.

The basement was almost completed. Nate suggested they go and see if the mayor would let them have or trade for some of the furniture and beds in the furniture warehouse they had been living in before.

"That's a great idea," said Steve. "Tomorrow we can take a Hummer into town and ask him."

"I'll go with you," said Craig. "I've been wondering how those guys and the others across the river have been doing."

"Five of us will go then," said Steve. "If he agrees to let us get the stuff we need then we can come back and get a tractor and trailer."

"I saw a lowboy trailer at the other end of the airstrip," said Joe. "I'll see if it's in working order, then we could fit all we need in one trip."

"Why don't we stop early today and take a much needed break," said James. "We can start on the hide room up top in the morning."

"Simon needs the next hangar over converted soon to house the new animals he's growing," said Steve. "That's a future project, but we do need to get it done before winter."

"How will we be feeding these animals?" asked Ray.

"I'll recon the area with the UAV," said Craig. "I'm sure there're some fields around here that we can harvest from."

It was early afternoon when they all stopped working, but everyone had been putting in long hours and it was nice to take a break and relax. They still had no perimeter breaches and were glad for it. The signs would hopefully help to ward off anyone that might want to scavenge in the area.

The next morning, the group assembled to go into the city and everyone else continued working on transforming their new home.

The Hummer drove up to the main gate. Joe got out, disarming the claymore attached to it. He opened the gate and let the Hummer drive through. He locked the gate and took the safety pin back out of the mine. He got back in and Craig navigated the mine field then continued into the city.

The precautions were thought necessary by most everyone in the group. There was always someone with a different or better idea than the rest, but the military minds always won out.

As they drove into downtown, people were stopping and staring at them.

"Does anyone else think this is strange?" asked Craig.

"I think we can all agree that something isn't right," said Steve. "Sam, keep an eye out up there will you?"

"I sure will," said Sam from the turret.

The Hummer finally got to the courthouse and they all got out except for Sam. He decided to stay with the vehicle because of how everyone was acting. The other men went inside to find the mayor.

A man that they had not seen before met them inside. They asked for the mayor. They were suddenly surrounded by armed men. The four men spread out to cover more area.

"I'm the mayor," said the man, who was short, skinny and bald, "how can I help you?"

"You are not," said Steve. "We're looking for Daniel."

"He was voted out of office, I'm Mayor Sinclair. How may I help you?"

"Well," said Craig, "if you are the man now then what would it take for us to get a few couches and beds from the abandoned furniture store?"

"It depends," said the mayor. "What do you have to trade?"

"We can offer you food," said Steve.

"How about some ammo for those weapons on your sides?" he said.

The men went into town with just side arms instead of full gear. They figured it would be safe to do so. They were saved by a burst of fire from the .50 Cal mounted on top the Hummer. They all ran out to see a crowd surrounding it. The people saw the other men coming back and dispersed.

The men opened the doors of the Hummer and Sam covered them as they entered.

"I want weapons and ammo for the furniture," said the new mayor as the men entered the Hummer.

"Like hell," said Steve as he got into the passenger side. Craig got in and they drove away.

"The other side of the river has taken over I see," said Craig. "I knew it would end this way."

"I think we all did," said Steve.

They headed back to talk to everyone and discuss what to do. They knew they could gut the trailers for beds, but if they could get access to the warehouse then they could get tables and couches too. They really didn't want to give their potential enemy weapons and ammo, but would if they really needed to. These things they wanted were just comforts, but why not have them if you can, everyone said.

The frame of the hide room covering the basement entrance was up and the walls were being started when they returned.

"How did it go?" asked James as the men got out of the Hummer.

"Not the way we had hoped," said Steve. "The mayor we met when we got here has been replaced by another man. He doesn't want food, he wants guns and ammo."

"Did you tell him no?" asked Karen as she walked up.

"We didn't tell him anything," said Craig, "we just left."

"We can't arm more people," said Nancy as she walked into the conversation.

"I know we can't," said Steve, "but this is a barter type of a world now and maybe we can offer them very little. They don't know what we have."

Hans was talking to Craig after they got back. "I should have stayed with Daniel," said Hans.

"If you had stayed, you might not be around either brother," said Craig.

"I could have protected him, I know it."

"Nothing you can do about it now, let's just focus on the future and keep each other alive," said Craig.

The discussion continued and they finally decided to give them two rifles, 100 rounds of ammo each and some food in return for the furniture that they weren't even using. The same group would go back into town in almost full gear to show them that they had very little.

They pulled one of the tractors out of the hangar. The lowboy trailer that they found was operational and they attached it to the tractor. They planned on making some kind of a deal before they came back. Two Hummers would go into the city this time. A kind of show of force was the idea. They only wanted beds and couches, but if someone wanted something bad enough, they would pay whatever they had to in this new world.

This time as they rolled up on the courthouse, there were more armed men outside. The civilians that were all over the street last time were nowhere to be seen now.

Craig and Steve got out of the lead Hummer and approached the new mayor as he walked out of the building.

"We've brought some things to bargain with," said Steve. "Can we go to the warehouse and talk?"

"I'll go with you and we'll see if we can reach an agreement," said the mayor.

He got in the Hummer with them and they went to the warehouse.

"Tell your men to stay out here," said Sinclair. "You come with me." He pointed at Steve. "Leave your weapons here."

Steve did as requested and followed the man inside. The warehouse had a few dozen armed men in it as well.

"Are you expecting company?" asked Steve.

"Let's just say that if you want it, there is a reason and it needs to be protected just like any investment," said Sinclair.

Steve picked out twelve beds, six couches, four dining room tables with chairs and seven recliners.

"Big family," said Sinclair.

"We have a few people in the group," said Steve. "Now what would you like for all of this stuff that doesn't belong to you?" asked Steve.

"Easy now," said Sinclair. "I'm the mayor and this does belong to me. I want a rifle for each piece and five hundred rounds of ammo each to go along with them. Also, ten clips with each."

"I will give you two rifles, one hundred rounds of ammo and two magazines each as well as a few months of food for you and your men," said Steve.

Sinclair was shaking his head. "Steve, Steve, Steve, I know you're sitting on a lot of weapons and ammo and I think you need to share with us."

"We're not sitting on, as you say, a lot of guns and ammo. We have a small arsenal that was depleted on our way here from Montana," said Steve. "Who else is going to want this stuff? What we are offering is a good deal for both of us. You can take it or leave it."

Steve turned around and started to walk away.

"Wait," said Sinclair.

Men pointed their weapons at Steve.

"Are you going to shoot me?" asked Steve. "Your men will all die if you do and you know it."

"We are bartering, are we not?" asked Sinclair as he motioned for his men to lower their weapons. "I will give you half of what you want for what you offer. If you want the other half, then you can bring the same to trade. Is this fair?"

Steve acted like he was thinking about it and finally said, "Okay. Have your men bring it out and put in on the trailer and I will get your stuff," said Steve.

Sinclair clapped his hands. The garage door opened up and the men started to carry the furniture out.

Steve told Craig over the radio to get the supplies for them. Ray and Craig brought the guns and ammo over and Sam and Nate brought the food. The mayor didn't look very happy about the trade, but it was better than nothing.

The trailer was loaded and the group left as fast as they could.

"Let's not do that again if we can avoid it," said Joe over the radio.

"I agree," said Steve. "This furniture will just about do it. Let's stop by that carpet store on the way out of town and see if we can get anything there."

The trucks stopped in front of the store and went in through the broken windows in the front. With no one in the building, they helped themselves to what they needed. The basement would look almost like home now.

Chapter Six: Home and the Range

The basement construction was complete and everyone was living in the new quarters. There was no bathroom down below, and only a small one in the hangar. If this was going to be home then the trailers could be modified, they thought. They decided on one trailer for showers and the other for bathrooms. They would have to scavenge what they needed from the city. They would try to stay clear of the part with the new mayor and his goons. They would focus on the part of the city that had little or no activity. There were many houses that people no longer lived in because they were either dead or moved into the city.

"We need to have a range day when we are finished with everything," said Nancy. "Joe said when we got out into the world again, I could shoot my shotgun and other weapons."

"She's right," said Joe, "I did say that. We've just been so busy trying to stay alive that I forgot. I'll put something together with some of the other guys and we'll have a nice range for all of us to use in a short time."

"We can use the dirt from digging the trench with the bobcat to make a berm," said Ray.

"Perfect," said Joe. "See Nancy, we'll be on the range in no time."

Nancy walked away smiling.

Water was starting to become a concern, so Craig was tasked with finding a drilling rig for drilling a well. Chris had a massive storage tank for them to use, but agreed that they would eventually need more too. Craig found an old phone book and after finding a few names and addresses, he put a team together to find what they needed.

The men Craig had chosen left in a Hummer to go find a drill truck for the well and hopefully the well driller. A farm close to the power plant was the first place he wanted to go. When the Hummer pulled up to the house an older man with short gray hair and coveralls on came out with a shotgun. The men got out to talk to him and he fired into the air.

"You boys can just get right back in that thing and leave," said the old man. "We don't have anything else you need."

"We're sorry to bother you sir," said Craig, "but we are looking for the well driller. We aren't here to take anything."

"You're looking for the well driller for what?" asked the old man.

"Well, to drill a water well sir," said Craig. "We're not here to hurt anyone; we're here to hire the well driller. Is he here?"

"That would be me son," said the old man, putting down his shotgun.

The man walked down from the porch and reached out his hand.

"My name's Bill; and you are?"

"Craig, sir, and this is Ray, Sam and Sven."

"Nice to meet you boys, where are you from? Did you just move here?"

"Ray and I are from the Billings area and these two live here," said Craig.

"Sorry for the shotgun," said Bill. "Things have gotten out of hand here lately."

"We understand," said Craig. "Now about the well sir."

"Yes," said Bill. "If you can get my truck running then we can talk business. I've tinkered on it for the last two years and can't figure out what's wrong with it."

"With the EMP that hit," said Ray, "it's probably just your solenoid. We can get it replaced, put some fresh fuel in it, and we should be able to get it running in no time."

"That would be great," said Bill.

The men got the information they needed from the truck and headed back into town. They stopped by a few mechanic shops until they found what they needed. The man inside the shop was more than happy to take some food for the parts.

Ray got the drill truck running after awhile and Bill was very happy.

"What will you need from us to drill a well?" asked Craig.

"Can I think about it?" asked Bill. "Just getting the truck running can be part of it, how's that sound?"

"Sounds good," said Craig. "When can you start?"

"Why don't we just go out to your house now?" asked Bill. "I have no other pressing business. Margret!" he yelled.

Out of the house came an old woman, slightly hunched over and appeared to have had a hard life, but could still move pretty fast. Her mouth was shrunken in like she had forgotten her dentures. "What?" she asked.

"We have a well to drill, get your work clothes on," said Bill.

She walked back in the house and came out a few minutes later with a pair of greasy coveralls on and got in the driver,s side of the truck.

"Follow us," said Craig.

The two trucks left the farm and rolled down the road toward the airstrip. The drill truck had a trailer behind it with well casing. When they got close to the gate, the Hummer stopped and Ray got out. He went up to the truck and explained to Bill about the minefield for security and asked if he could drive. Bill had Margret get out and get in the Hummer. The trucks made it through and drove up to the back side of the big hangar. Everyone got out, and Bill looked around wide-eyed.

"You folks live here?" he asked.

"It's a long story," said Craig. "I'll go and get the engineers for you to talk to about the well."

Steve and James came out of the back door and walked over to the drill truck.

Craig introduced everyone and the men started talking about working out a deal. After listening to everything, Bill said, "How about I drill you this well and Margret and I live here in this well protected place you have. Now just hear me out boys, I can tell you want to say something. We will maintain the well and keep it drinkable. We will help out wherever else you need us to. We've been living on a farm with no more livestock and barely surviving. We have more and more bandits coming around and won't last much longer I fear."

Steve and James looked at each other, and Craig butted in.

"You have hay fields don't you?" asked Craig.

"Well it's a farm son," said Bill, "so yes I do but they haven't been producing and it would take some work on the fields and the equipment. Why do you ask?"

"We have farm animals being grown right now," said Steve, "and they will need food. I think we can come to an arrangement for you and your wife. Please let us know if you need anything or any help. We thank you for coming to our aid."

"Farm animals being grown, from what?" asked Bill.

"We have a scientist that has frozen embryos of animals and is growing them so we can have food," said James.

Bill and Margret stared strangely at each other for a minute, shrugged their shoulders and then got to work on the well. Everyone else got back to work too.

The perimeter had still not been breached, but they were all ready for when it happened, because they knew it would eventually.

The range was under construction and Nancy was excited about going shooting. She knew it would be good for everyone to take a break from all of the hard work and do something enjoyable. The work kept everyone busy, but they needed a change, even for a short time.

The kids had been a big help, but were getting tired of every day being filled with work and no play. They could be found hiding in different places all the time avoiding the work.

"We will have everything built soon and there will be less to do," Karen told all of them in a meeting about listening and duties, which the women put together just for them.

More and more items were checked off of the 'To-Do Board' as Sherri called it. The time had finally come to go to the range. Everything was set up one morning in preparation for the day. Joe picked out four different weapons that most had expressed interest in shooting.

Safety rules were brought up again and a re-familiarization of the weapons given. Only a certain amount of ammo was brought out of the new armory. With no way to build the ammo reserves back up at this point, it was a good idea. Everyone was accounted for and the targets started to get shot up. The fundamentals that they had all been taught the whole time underground came together as they fired at the targets. They were only shooting the rifles at a hundred yards away, but even the combat vets were impressed with the grouping the novice shooters were hitting. They all did equally well with the handguns.

Steve had invited Chris and his group, but they didn't show up until they were almost done shooting. A ceasefire was called and the others were given instructions and told the safety rules. Chris and most of his group fired the weapons that were at the range. Some didn't want to shoot at all, and just had fun watching.

Everyone had fun. Kim was taking pictures of them all for what she called the archives, which she was putting together. She said she would get Steve's book to put in with them also once he was done with it. A picnic type dinner was planned for after the shooting day at the new range. A barbeque would have been better, but they had no grill and no fresh meat yet to put on one. They knew it was just a matter of time until they had some, as long as Simon's plan worked. Ray said he would build a grill for when the time came that they had some to put on it.

"How's the jet coming along?" Steve asked Chris.

"It is a slow and methodical process," he said. "We want to make sure it flies and doesn't fall from the sky once we are up there."

"Yes," said Steve with a smile, "that would be bad."

"What are your plans once you get it ready?" asked Craig.

"We want to go to our other bunkers and get supplies," said Chris. "We're adding extra fuel tanks just in case we can't land and re-fuel."

"We should find some parachutes," said Craig. "If you can't land and it's not real bad on the ground, you can have a few people jump and clear the landing strip."

"I like that idea," said Chris. "Are you volunteering to jump for us?"

"I would be more than happy to talk to you about doing that," said Craig. "After all, we are neighbors."

"Thank you for inviting us," said Kerri. "We've been underground for so long that I forgot what it was like out here."

"Your girls look like they're having fun with the other kids," said Maria. "You know that they are very safe up here and can come and hang out anytime right?"

"The offer is well received," said Chris. "We're lucky to have such good neighbors."

Craig looked over and the men nodded.

The evening was wrapped up and everyone went their separate ways.

The next morning, an explosion woke most everyone. Even Chris and his people were awakened by their world rocking like an earthquake had hit. The reaction team on duty for the week got up, putting all of their gear on in no time to go and meet the threat. Two Hummers raced toward the main gate and saw a few people wading through the mine field. Behind them were men in vehicles with guns yelling at them.

Jake got on a loud speaker he had found in one of the hangars and told the people to stop walking or they would die. They stopped and a woman was shot by one of the men on the other side. She fell to the ground and set off another mine.

"I count sixteen men," said Ray.

"They're telling the people to walk through to set off the mines," said Hans. "We should take them out."

"We could hit the people in the middle," said Jake. "Ray, carefully get on some night vision and tell me where the mines are. Can they make it?"

"One of them is walking straight for one," said Ray.

"Cover me!"

Jake ran toward the gate yelling for them to stop. He all of a sudden felt like he hit a brick wall and everything went blurry. A firefight ensued and Jake lay motionless in the dirt.

The vehicles on the other side exploded as the Hummers' .50 cal rounds tore through them. None of the men over there survived. There was only one woman and one small girl left alive in the mine field when it was all over. They were told to lay still until someone could get to them. Gary and Trevor were called to attend to the wounded. There was blood all around Jake's head. Hans and a few other men went to get the two survivors and check on the others that had started the fighting. Ray was holding Jakes head with a shirt when Gary got to him.

"Let me see," said Gary.

Trevor went to see if anyone else needed attention.

Jake had been hit in the side of the head with a bullet. It had only grazed him, but it was enough to knock him unconscious and cause him to bleed badly.

Gary stabilized Jake and a Hummer took him back to the hangar and to the medical center that had been built inside.

The fires from the exploding vehicles were put out with fire extinguishers and the area was searched. The bodies of the dead were put in one pile to be buried. The weapons and ammo that could be salvaged were collected. The mine field was searched and pieces were picked up so they weren't mistaken later for other mines. The woman and child were taken to the medical center to be looked at. When Trevor got back, he got a few volunteers to give blood for Jake. He decided at that point to get a separate cooler to store extra blood in for times like these. It would be his next project.

Jake started having a seizure and had to be watched so he didn't fall off of the table. Holding him down might make things worse. It was late morning when all the excitement finally died down. A late breakfast was made, but a few people didn't feel like eating.

"We need to find out what that was all about," said Steve to everyone as they ate.

"I will go and talk to the woman," said Sherri.

With Sherri's negotiating skills, she should could likely get the information the group needed or at least tell whether the woman was lying or telling the truth.

Jake had stabilized again but was still unconscious. He would need to be monitored constantly. A rotation was set up for this.

That evening, Sherri went to talk to the woman.

"Hi there," said Sherri. "What's your name?" she asked the little girl.

"Lizzy," she said.

"How old are you?" asked Sherri.

"I'm six, what's your name?"

"My name is Sherri. What were you and your mommy doing out there today?"

"Those men told us to walk," said Lizzy.

"Leave her alone," said the woman.

"I was wondering if you were going to join the conversation," said Sherri. "Is she your daughter?"

"Yes," said the woman.

"What is your name?" asked Sherri.

"Why are you keeping us here?" asked the woman.

"Why were those men sending you out to die?" asked Sherri.

"I don't know, leave us alone."

Sherri left as the woman requested and vowed to try again in the morning. The people watching Jake would watch the woman and Lizzy too. They could leave the next day if they wanted, but were welcomed to stay also. Trevor thought the woman was still in shock.

Jake stayed the same throughout the night. The woman and her daughter finally went to sleep. James woke up the next morning to people talking. He must have dozed off. Lizzy was talking with a still unconscious Jake. James started to record the conversation on his cell phone camera. He knew no one would believe him. He kept recharging the phone and kept it in his pocket just in case he wanted to take a picture or to try to hold on to what was lost.

Gary walked into the room and saw Lizzy next to Jake. He looked at James and walked over to Jake to see how he was doing.

"You won't believe this," said James.

James showed Gary the recording and Gary was flabbergasted.

Jake had been talking and answering Lizzy's questions while he lay there sleeping.

The woman woke up too, with all the commotion. She seemed in a better state of mind as Gary examined her. She even said her name was Nicole. She and her daughter had just been walking down the street in the city to try and find some food when the men grabbed them. They told everyone that they would shoot them if they didn't walk toward the fence. Nicole thanked everyone in the room for saving her and her daughter. She accepted their hospitality and the chance at a new life.

Chapter Seven: Contact

"I don't know why you keep wasting time with that radio Allie," said Carl.

She had tried to get someone to answer her calls for weeks since they had all come out of the bunkers and moved onto the airstrip. James had shown her how to use the radio once he had put the array together.

"I will get someone; just you wait and see Carl." Allie kept trying as he walked away.

"Hello, hello who is this?" said a faint and garbled voice.

Carl stopped right where he was. "Where is that coming from?" he asked.

"Quiet, said Allie. This is Allie Longmire."

"Don't tell them your name!" said Carl.

"Shhhh," she said. Allie kept trying to tune the radio to get better reception. By this time, more people had gathered around the table to listen.

"This is Doug Stockton aboard the International Space Station, can you hear me?" His voice came in loud and clear.

"Yes, yes we can," said Allie.

"Where are you?" he asked.

Allie looked around for confirmation and got a nod from an older man whose name she suddenly forgot in all the excitement.

"We are survivors living in Idaho. Are you really on the space station?" she asked.

"Yes we are," said Doug.

Everyone started to cheer and Allie had to quiet them down.

"We are about to pass the cchchchhchch." Doug broke up and Allie kept trying to get him back.

They all slowly walked away. Allie wouldn't leave; she knew she could get him back. Three hours passed and then a high-pitched noise came back on the radio and she could hear Doug again.

"What happened?" she asked.

"We had to slow the station down in order to stay directly above you in geosynchronous orbit. This had to be done slowly or risk tearing this old thing in half or worse."

"How long have you been up there?" asked Allie.

"Our shuttle left earth just days before the bombs fell. We were part of a few different missions to figure out a way to bring life back to a dying earth. There are other teams underground too."

"That's where we were," said Allie.

"We watched as the earth was destroyed, or so we thought, until we started to pick up your radio transmissions just recently. The planet was knocked off of its original axis and our instruments had to be recalibrated to compensate," said Doug.

"This is incredible," said Allie.

James had walked into the communications room after he got the word that Allie was talking to someone. He listened to the conversation and then asked if he could talk to Doug.

"Hi Doug, this is James. Can we get some kind of confirmation that you are who you say you are? I want to believe you, but you have to understand after all that has happened that we need to be cautious."

"I understand," said Doug. "I can't give you anything but my word right now. We will need a place to land and if you and your people are willing, we can come back to earth in your area if there is an airstrip long enough."

"How long does it need to be?" asked James.

"The airstrip at the Kennedy space center is fifteen thousand feet long, but we don't need that much room. How much do you have at the nearest strip to you? It would be nice to have radio contact upon reentry too," said Doug.

"I will have to get back to you on that," said James. "If we lose contact, can we get you back later?"

"Yes, we should be able to talk just about any time," said Doug.

"Great, I will let you know as soon as I can find out," said James.

James went to find Steve and then go talk to Chris about the length of the landing strip.

The two men went to the next hangar over to talk to Chris. All the doors were locked, so they started banging on them. Finally Ben came and opened a door.

"What's going on guys?" asked Ben. "Is everything okay?"

"We need to talk to Chris and find out how long this airstrip is," said Steve.

Ben opened the door and let them in. The jet was coming together nicely. Chris walked up to them. "How can I help you guys today?" he asked.

James told them about Allie talking on the radio and getting in touch with a man that said he was on the International Space Station. They needed a place to land the shuttle and needed radio contact to do so.

"You're right," said Chris. "It does sound like someone is just messing with the girl. If he is telling the truth, then they may need a longer strip than this one. It's barely seven thousand feet long. I don't know that they will stop before they reach the end."

"Will you guide them in if they decide to land here?" asked James. "You're the closest person to an air traffic controller we have."

"I can do that if this is real," said Chris. "When do they want to land?"

"We just started talking to them," said James.

"Preparations can be made for the landing," said Chris. "A longer strip would be nice, but this one will work as long as there is a good pilot behind the stick. The shuttle is a glider and the flaps will only slow it down so much. There is no guarantee that the parachute will deploy either. We can put a large net across the landing strip to considerably slow them down if not stop them completely. I can go and talk to the pilot if you want me to."

"That would be great," said James.

They all left and went to the large hangar to talk to the man that said he was in space. It all sounded just a little strange, but they would find out the truth soon. Chris knew stuff to ask the man and would know if he was for real.

When they got to the communications room, Allie was still talking to Doug. James asked her if they could talk to him and she said goodbye.

"Doug, this is James again. I have a pilot that wants to talk to you."

"Go ahead."

"Hi Doug, this is Chris. How are you guys doing up there? Have you had any problems with solar flares or increases in radiation?"

"We have been pretty lucky so far with SMEs," said Doug.

"Great," said Chris. "Have you or anyone else had any issues with, asthenia?"

"No," said Doug, "we have not had any anyone depressed, hypersensitive or wanting to go on a murderous rampage lately. Look, I know what you are getting at and I assure you that we are up here and I am Doug Stockton. Can you put Allie back on the radio? I was having a more intellectual conversation with her."

"I think we can safely say that they are up there," said Chris to the others.

"Thanks for humoring me Doug. I hope you understand that we need to know who we are dealing with. I can help you bring your glider back to earth when you're ready. How many are you up there?"

"We are four," said Doug, "and we will be coming down in the Shuttle Enterprise."

"We will stay in contact," said Chris.

"Thanks Chris and yes I understand completely. We'll watch the weather patterns from up here and let you know when we're ready," said Doug.

"Sounds good," said Chris. "We will prep the landing area, and we'll need some time to rig up a trap too. I'm not completely satisfied with the amount of room you'll have."

"Sounds like a plan," said Doug.

"What's an SME?" asked Kim as Chris got off the radio.

"A solar mass ejection, a solar flare for short," said Chris.

"You learn something new every day," said Kim, "thanks."

Allie got back on the radio and continued to talk to the astronaut. Everyone got together to plan what they needed to do to prep for the shuttle's arrival.

"We will need to take down the trip wires and recover the mines at the end of the airstrip," said Craig. "We don't want them to explode when they land if they go too far."

"Agreed," said Steve. "We'll do that two days prior to their arrival. Where can we find netting for the trap Chris?"

"We will have to look in the hangars for cargo netting. If we can't find enough, we'll have to go look in other areas of the city unfortunately. If we're going to do this, then we have a narrow window of about five to six weeks before it cools off and might be too icy for them to land."

A few projects were put on hold in order to get ready for the landing of the space shuttle. Everyone was excited about the landing. Those in the shuttle saw everything from up above a couple of years before and could hopefully give some insight into what really happened and possibly why.

Craig wanted to find out more about who attacked and why, but it would have to wait. More important items had to be handled first.

The well was drilled and ready for a pump house. Ray and a couple of men took this project on, as it was also a priority. The trailers had been converted for the bathrooms and shower rooms. Shower stalls and toilets had been rounded up from the surrounding area for the retrofitting. Once the water was ready, they could be used. Tanks for grey water would also be needed. A dumpsite would need to be established and a burn pit too. With all the work, many people needed a shower. Proper hygiene was put on the back burner due to the seriousness of all the projects, but it couldn't be put off for long. Gary and Trevor stressed the need for it and helped out where they could too.

Constant contact was made with the space station; it was usually Allie that was on the radio. She had found a new passion. Chris and the guys kept working on reassembling the jet. At one point, Steve asked why they didn't just piece one together from the other jets around the airstrip. The one that Chris owned was a modified version of a Biz Jet, he told them. It would take longer to retrofit one that was already assembled to be like his.

Sherri was happy with the progress that everyone had made in such a short time. Many projects had been finished and crossed out on the board.

Cargo netting was found in abundance in a hangar near the northern perimeter. The men thought they had enough to cover the entire width of the airstrip. They would have to make anchors as well to put on both sides. Bill and Margret would drill holes on each side with their drill truck to put the anchors deeper than they could have with anything else. Nate found a welder and a few guys helped out to make it operational. The trap project would be done in no time.

One evening after dinner, Craig sent the UAV up just to look at the area. He noticed that there had been more foot activity outside the fence in one certain part of the perimeter.

"The people around the air strip must be getting more curious as to what we're doing here," Craig said to Bill as they sat in lawn chairs they had found.

"They have got to be starving out there," said Bill.

"Well they can't have our food," said Craig as he flew the Switchblade back to earth.

"Can I try it?" asked Chris as he walked up.

"I don't know," said Craig. "Are you certified on this particular aircraft?"

"I feel confident that I can fly it," said Chris with a smile. "Does that count?"

"Okay," said Craig. "Just don't scratch it and have it back soon."

Chris sent the UAV back up in the air. He started to ask Craig about the small remote plane. What the flying time was, the range and other features. Bill went back inside the hangar to see what Theresa was doing. They hadn't told anyone, but the way they were acting around each other, a few people in the group picked up on it. Craig and Chris stayed outside until almost dark.

The next day James made contact with Doug again and the two men coordinated the landing with Chris. The weather had been clear with little to no wind. It was the end of August and still pretty hot out. From the view aboard the space station, there were no storms approaching. The astronauts made final preparations in the shuttle.

Within a few days, they would be streaking across the sky and hopefully landing without any problems.

After dinner that night, a meeting was called with everyone that now lived in the hangar compound.

"Thanks for showing up everyone," said Steve.

Even Chris and his group were there.

"We have all in our own ways overcome so much in the last couple of years. Some more than others, but we have all been there for each other. Some of us have been together since the beginning; some have recently joined the group. I for one am glad to call all of you my friends," said Steve.

"Tomorrow we will be joined by four more people. They have been in zero gravity longer than anyone in history. They will be weak and will need our help," said Steve. "Does anyone have any questions?"

No hands were raised, so Steve turned the floor over to Sherri.

"I know everyone is tired from all of the hard work," said Sherri, "so I will be quick. As you can see on the board behind me, most of the projects have been completed. We have some new ideas right here and when we can, they will be open for discussion. Good news, for those of you that don't know, the bathrooms are open for service and have been used already. The showers that some of you have been working so hard on are finished as well. Please limit your time in the shower, we have plenty of water, but there are many of you and only six of them and limited hot water until we can get more electric hot water heaters converted. We will plan on adding another trailer when there is time. I have put together a roster and would like you all to follow it. I did not discriminate, so please just be happy with what you have. Does anyone have any questions for me?"

A few people raised their hands and the questions were answered either by Sherri or others. Everyone was satisfied and went off to take showers and get some rest for the exciting day that lay ahead.

Chris approached Steve and offered their showers to the people with families.

"We have plenty of water and you know we have the room," said Chris.

A few people took Chris's offer and went into the bunker to wash up. It would have taken hours to get through everyone if they had all used the new showers.

The kids were having fun in the old silo after they had taken their showers. A few of the girls stayed the night with Silvia and Rachel.

The shuttle re-entry was scheduled for landing at 9 a.m. the next morning and would be seen for over a hundred square miles, or possibly further, as it approached. They all hoped that it didn't bring people in looking for what came out of the sky. They all tried to get some sleep, but the excitement kept some people up.

The next morning was an early one for most. The last bit of preparations had to be made in order to get the shuttle down safely. With no computers to calculate trajectory or approach angle, it would be up to the pilot to bring the bird in. No emergency vehicles would be waiting on the ground to put out fires or to help the astronauts if they crashed.

Everyone had their assignments and got them done as quickly as they could. Everything was double and triple checked. Chris made contact with Doug. As everything entered the final stages, the tension was rising. The shuttle had separated from the station and was moving into position for the re-entry. They were talking to the ground through all the sequences. It would all take time and the waiting made it worse for some.

"We are firing the RCS thrusters now," came a woman's voice over the radio.

"Roger that Enterprise," said Chris.

Chris told everyone what was happening while the shuttle positioned itself.

"They are turning the shuttle over and going tail first," said Chris.

"We are now firing the OMS engines," said the woman's voice again.

"They are now slowing the shuttle down for the fall back to earth," said Chris. "This will take about twenty-five minutes. They will then be in the upper atmosphere. They will be firing the RCS thrusters soon so they can pitch the shuttle over and the bottom will be facing the atmosphere and moving nose first again. We will be out of radio contact for approximately twelve minutes because of ionization blackout. They are moving at about seventeen thousand miles an hour at this point," said Chris.

"How do you know so much about this?" asked Allie.

"You know those companies that were going to be taking people into space as tourists?" asked Chris.

"I think so," said Allie.

"Well, I owned one of those companies," said Chris.

"Explains a lot," said Steve.

"I couldn't just offer all the answers right off the bat," said Chris. "I have as much to lose if not more than you in this world we now call home."

"I understand completely," said Steve.

The radio had static coming from it.

"We should be able to see them very soon," said Chris.

Some of them left the communications room and went outside to join the rest of the people that were already out there.

They could soon see a fireball streaking across the sky and heard a sonic boom. The fireball went away after a few minutes. It had cleared the Rocky Mountains and was losing altitude. The space shuttle was on final approach for the old air strip.

"Did it crash?" asked one of the kids.

"No, it just slowed down and leveled out," said Nate. "Here, look through my binoculars."

"I see it," she said.

"Everyone get ready, here it comes," said James.

As the shuttle glided in for its landing, everyone's mouths were wide open in awe. It zigzagged across the sky. It was explained later that they had to do that in order to slow down. The shuttle continued to glide and lose more altitude. The landing gear popped out from the underside, which helped slow it down too. The shuttle moved into position and then touched down on the airstrip. It started to slow even more when the parachute deployed. The chute stayed open for less than thirty seconds and then broke off. As it broke off, the force shot the nose forward and then the front landing gear broke. The nose fell to the ground and made an awful noise. Sparks were flying off the shuttle and it didn't seem to help it slow down. The shuttle skidded for a few hundred yards before stopping in the net trap at the end of the tarmac. Everyone waited until the dust cleared to approach it. Most of them had to walk to the end of the airstrip. There wasn't enough room in the Hummers and the astronauts would have to ride back to the hangar because they wouldn't be able to walk.

Steve stopped on the way up to the shuttle and was staring.

"What's wrong?" asked Karen. "Steve, Steve?"

"Yes, I'm sorry what was the question?" he asked.

"What are you staring at?"

"Nothing, I just had a very strange feeling like someone was talking to me," said Steve.

"Nobody said anything," said Karen, "until you just stopped."

They continued to walk toward the shuttle with Karen looking at Steve strangely.

The astronauts had been in the International Space Station for more than two years and wouldn't be able to walk for many reasons. Being weightless for so long has an adverse effect on a person's bone structure and doesn't allow for the proper growth of cells. The people on the ground knew they would have to open the doors and help them get out. Chris told everyone that it would be about twenty minutes before the crew would be done powering the shuttle down. The outside would be very hot for a while too. The group waited for a little longer and they were almost to the front of the shuttle when the front left hatch popped off with a small explosion. The people that happened to be armed at this point pulled their weapons and pointed them in the direction of the sound. This was just a natural reaction, and they soon holstered and lowered them. A yellow rubber slide came out and started to air up. They saw a figure at the door and then another. They were standing on their own. Four people came down the slide and stood before them. They all had bags with them. They had backpacks and some had laptop cases.

"How are you able to walk?" asked Chris, as he approached them.

They were not only walking, but they all looked young, in their twenties.

"We took a gene therapy that was designed aboard the space station. It allows our tissue to heal faster," said a female astronaut.

"What on earth have you people been doing up there?" asked James.

"Research, it's what we have always done up there and it has paid off many times, just as it did this time." Everyone started to introduce themselves to the astronauts.

"We are so glad to finally meet all of you," said Jim Tanner, the co-pilot. "We've been talking to you for months and I'm very happy we made it."

"So are we," said Chris.

"It was a close call there for a minute or so. This isn't the type of airstrip we usually land this baby on," said Jim.

Everyone loaded up in the Hummers for the ride back to the hangar. On the way, the lead truck had to stop suddenly and out came one of the astronauts, Ann, a tall woman with long blonde hair. She bent over and vomited. When she was done, she got back in the Hummer and they continued on.

When they got inside the hangar, they all got out and the astronauts started looking around and asking questions.

"Nice place you have here," said Jim. "I didn't know you actually lived on the airfield."

"I thought I told you that," said Chris smiling.

"Can I have everyone calm down?" asked Steve. "I know this is very exciting, but our new guests need to be debriefed, you could say, so can everyone please find something to do. We will all get a chance to get to know them if they want to stay."

They all reluctantly went about their days work on projects. The astronauts were taken to the communications room.

Chapter Eight: Getting Acquainted

"Does anyone want something to drink?" asked James.

"I'll take a beer," said Jim.

"Soda," said Jillian.

"I will see what I can find," said Nate.

Chris stopped him on his way out of the room and told him to go and talk to Ben.

"I'm still astounded at how you are able to walk," said Steve.

"As I told you," said Jillian, "we developed a gene therapy that allows us to heal faster."

"Would you mind if our doctors look you over after we talk?" asked James.

"Not at all," said Doug.

Nate walked back in after a little while with some beer, whisky and some Pepsi.

The astronauts were very happy and continued to talk with the men for a couple of hours. When they were done, they all walked over to the medical room that had been recently built to meet Trevor and Gary.

"It's a pleasure to finally meet you," said Gary.

"It really is," said Trevor.

The doctors put the astronauts through a series of tests. With very little equipment available, it was nothing like they would have got from a regular test series.

"Would you like to see something even more amazing than us walking after so long in zero gravity?" asked Doug.

"Yes we would," said Gary.

"Do you have a scalpel handy?"

"Yes, over here," said Trevor.

"Why do you want a scalpel?" asked Gary.

"It will be better if I just show you, and not tell you," said Doug.

Doug took the scalpel from Trevor and then grabbed Ann from behind. "I'm sorry baby," he said, and slit her throat.

Ann slowly fell to the floor; there was blood everywhere.

Craig pulled his sidearm and pointed it at Doug. Everyone was yelling.

"Don't shoot!" yelled Steve as he got in front of Craig.

"What the hell are you doing?" asked Craig.

Everyone was standing there staring at Ann's body.

"Just wait," said Doug as he set the scalpel down on the counter and backed away.

Ann started coughing and started to get up. They all backed away as she stood up with Doug's help. The astronauts were smiling, but everyone else in the room was in awe.

"This was a demonstration of the gene therapy we mentioned," said Ann with a scratchy voice.

"Amazing," said Gary. "I need to... we all need to know more."

"We will share everything with only the pure of heart," said Jillian. "This power is not for everyone."

While Trevor was talking with Jim, he cut Jim's arm and it healed almost instantly.

"What else has the gene therapy done to you?" asked Steve.

"We haven't been able to put much else to the test," said Doug, "but I noticed right away when we exited the shuttle that I could hear much more and see much further."

"Do you have super strength?" asked Craig.

"Okay," said Gary. "We need to keep a lid on this. No one outside the room can know about any of what has happened. Trevor and I will coordinate with these fine people and run every test we can think of. Ann, I will get you some of my wife clothes. We can't have you walking around looking like that."

Ann smiled and thanked him.

A few more walls had been put up in the basement to make room for the new people. They were shown to their rooms, and after they got settled they would get the tour of the compound.

"How long have you been here?" asked Doug.

"Only a few months," said Steve as they walked downstairs to the living area.

"I find it amazing how quickly you have transformed everything to fit your needs."

"We are all about survival," said Steve. "We've had nothing to do but this."

"I suppose you're right," said Doug. "I'm still trying to adapt to the idea that everything I had or ever knew is gone."

"What did you leave behind?" asked Steve.

"A wife and kids, like most of us," said Doug. "Ann and I plan on starting a new family. Hers is gone now too more than likely."

"Do you have no hope that they made it and may still be alive?" asked James. "We survived as well as many other people."

"This is my life now and it would be great if they were alive, but I feel that I need to move on down this new path," said Doug.

The astronauts were very appreciative of the hospitality that they were given. Extra clothes from some members of the group had been donated to the newcomers. Four small rooms were to be made up, but as it turned out they only needed two. With so long away from anyone else and knowing that their families were more than likely gone, the four people had moved on. The confined space that they had lived in for years on the space station made the temptation even greater.

The testing would start the following day along with a guided tour of the whole area. Jim had seen the computers set up and book shelves with many books.

"What do you have over here?" Jim asked Steve as they walked through the living area.

"This is our library," said Steve. "Everyone's favorite books are available for the others to read. The computers can access anything in the servers. I put as much information as I could on them before the end."

"Then you must have terabytes of information?" asked Jim.

"Yes we do," said Steve. "As a collective, we brought to the bunkers everything we thought would help us rebuild after the apocalypse."

"You've done well," said Jim. "I'm looking forward to seeing everything else during the tour tomorrow. Would it be okay to tap into your servers if we needed to? With no Internet, this would be the closest thing."

"Feel free to use our computers, or your own while attached to ours," said Steve. "We have a very good selection of music and information on most subjects."

"I'm sorry about the lighting down here. We're working on getting more lights as soon as we can, but need to find some that haven't been damaged or in use already."

"I can actually see very well in the dark," said Jim. "We can do many things that you can't."

Steve was even more intrigued with their abilities.

Security that night had been put on a higher alert level because of the landing and the new people and their abilities. The end of the airstrip had no trip wires or mines protecting it. Those would be put back into action the next day. The Hummers with men in them were sitting in front of the main hangar in case they needed to react to a threat; they would be able to react faster.

Luckily, the night was uneventful. The astronauts were up very early the next morning and were running on the airstrip. The men in the tower could not believe how fast they were running. The reaction team manning the Hummers went out to watch also.

"How the hell are they doing that?" Jake asked Joe.

"I have no idea man," said Joe.

"This is incredible," said Nate. "Weren't we told they shouldn't even be able to walk?"

"That's what I remember, too," said Bill as he walked over from his Hummer.

The four new people ran over to the Hummers and looked like they had barely broken a sweat. They were not breathing hard either.

"Wow!" said Jill. "I forgot how exhilarating that was."

"I know what you mean," said Doug.

Sometime later, Gary walked out and saw the astronauts by the Hummers. He had heard what was going on.

"Good morning," said Gary. "Breakfast is almost done and then we can get to those tests."

"Great," said Jim. "I'm starving."

"Me too," said the others.

Everyone went inside to eat except for the tower watch. They would rotate out when their relief was done.

Word of the new people running very fast on the airstrip spread like wildfire among the people in the hangar. Everyone wanted to talk to them. Gary, however, had other plans. He got them into the medical facility as fast as he could once they were done eating.

"You guys are like celebrities out there," said Trevor.

"We're just new and they will all get to know us," said Ann.

One at a time, the astronauts were put through a series of tests to determine certain things. With very little equipment, however, Gary and Trevor couldn't do all that they wanted.

After they were all done, Gary asked, "Is there any ability that you have that is not apparent?"

"I can read your mind," said Ann.

"Please," said Gary with a smile, "go ahead and tell me what I'm thinking."

"You are thinking about a trip you went on with your parents when you were young, to Australia," said Ann.

"Incredible!" said Gary. "Can all of you do that?

"Just me," said Ann. "I believe it's because I'm pregnant."

"That would make sense," said Trevor. "With the addition of another mind, both would be stronger. Can you speak with the child in you?"

"It's early in his development," said Ann, "but yes I can hear emerging thoughts."

"You even know what the sex is," said Gary excitedly. "This is..."

"Incredible?" said Doug.

"Well yes," said Gary. "Can you show me your research or do you have a sample of the inoculation you used to enhance and modify your genome?"

"As I said, this is not for everyone," said Jillian.

"How will you know who will be able to benefit from this?" asked Trevor.

"We will let you know," said Ann.

The four of them left the medical center and Steve walked in. "Are you done with the testing already?" he asked.

"With no equipment really to use," said Gary, "we had only a few we could run that we didn't last night."

"Well with what you have then, what do you think?"

"They certainly can heal very fast," said Gary. "They all appear to look about twenty-five years old too.

"I noticed that," said Steve. "They can't be though, right?"

"No, according to Jim, he's fifty-six years old."

"So this stuff makes them younger and heal faster?" asked Steve.

"Hold on, that's not all. They have extremely good vision," said Trevor. "They can see better than we can with binoculars on fifteen power. That's better than fifteen times better than us. All of their senses are better; smell, hearing and touch also."

"Amazing," said Steve. "Are they willing to share this with us?"

"Not on a wide scale it sounds like," said Gary. "From what they were saying, they will choose who will get it. They also have a better one that they want to test underground for safety reasons."

"We need to know more," said Steve. "They seem have discovered the 'Fountain of Youth' for lack of a better term."

The men continued to talk about the gene therapy. The astronauts had gone outside for some fresh air. Steve and James soon joined them and asked if they were ready to hear their story and go on a tour of the compound.

"We've been waiting patiently," said Ann with a smile.

The group walked around to the different areas and Steve started telling them about how they built the bunkers and their life since then. The tour and conversation lasted a couple of hours. The last stop was Chris's missile silo-turned-bunker.

Chris welcomed all of them in and showed them the whole underground facility.

"I think this will do," said Jim.

"Yes, if you will let us perform our experiments down here," said Doug, "then it would be safer for everyone."

"What kind of experiments?" asked Chris.

"We want to continue with the experiments that we were conducting on the space station," said Doug. "We've found a way to enhance human genes and want to take it to the next level."

"We need a secure facility to do this," explained Ann.

"We would need all of you to leave of course," said Jim.

Chris, Kerri and the others looked at each other as if they didn't know what to say.

"Please think about it and let us know as soon as possible," said Doug.

"I was planning to leave once my jet is reassembled," said Chris. "We need to go and check on the other sites that I have."

"We would like to bring everything back here and consolidate it," said Ben.

"We can help you put the aircraft together," said Jim.

"We would welcome the help," said Chris.

"Can you tell us about your experiments and how they have helped you?" asked Kerri.

They all sat down and the kids left the room.

"The gene therapy is based on creating a twenty-fourth pair of chromosomes. Space was a good place for trials. If anything went wrong, there was nowhere to go. The other team that was working on this was placed deep underground for safety reasons as well. We had great success right away with no adverse reactions. We were also working on other things that could be more dangerous. We ran computer simulations and they worked in those. We need to be in an underground bunker in order to run human trials," said Jill.

"Where is the other test facility?" asked Gary.

"It's somewhere in Colorado, that's all we know," said Doug.

"What's so dangerous about the testing?" asked Chris.

"We have enhanced our abilities in every way imaginable," said Ann. "The next step would be basically super human, or even a new species. We could potentially be creating monsters if anything went wrong and need containment just in case things don't work out."

"So, the gene therapy the four of you took is just the standard one?" asked Sherri.

"Yes it is and it's incredible. I can see further, don't get fatigued and heal very fast," said Jill.

"Then you are better than the average human already?" asked Sherri.

"In a sense yes," said Jim.

"Then why would you need to be better than that?"

Chris changed the subject and Sherri glared at him.

"Can you demonstrate anything for us?" asked Chris.

"Do you have any steel rods?" asked Jill.

Ben went to get one and in the meantime, Doug asked for a knife.

"Doug, please don't make another mess," said Steve.

"I won't, but if I could show you in the kitchen maybe?"

They all followed Doug. Ben got back just in time for the demonstration. Doug put his arm over the sink and sliced his forearm open. It bled badly for a few seconds and healed right away. There were some gasps and wows.

Ann took the steel rod and asked Chris to bend it. Knowing that he couldn't, he tried anyway. Ann took it back from him and bent it like it was nothing.

"Incredible," said Sherri. "I just have to ask, why were you sent into space just days before the bombs fell? Did our government know this was going to happen?"

"I apologize," said Chris. "Life has been difficult to adjust to since the bombs fell."

"No need to," said Doug. "We were sent up there to perform many experiments and the gene therapy was just one of them. It was just a coincidence that nuclear war happened just days after we left. If we had known it was going to happen, most of us would not have got on the shuttle. We would have wanted to be with our families."

"We do hope that what we have gained from what has happened will only benefit human kind," said Ann.

"I will let you know about the use of the bunker," said Chris. "We all need to talk about it."

"Thank you for your hospitality and consideration," said Jim.

The new people left and went back up to the surface.

"This inoculation could mean a new beginning for humanity," said Chris. "They may have just attained immortality."

"I don't necessarily need to live forever," said Steve, "but to live without sickness or chronic fatigue. That would be incredible!"

Everyone continued to talk about the possibilities; and the thought of being stronger, faster and healing right away was fantastic.

"Will they share this gene therapy with us?" asked Sherri.

"The question was already brought up to them, and the answer was that it would not be for everyone," said Steve. "We will just have to wait and see."

Chapter Nine: Experiments

Live tissue samples were taken from everyone in the group that lived on the airfield. They were all tested for compatibility before they could be injected. A list of people that could have it was given to Steve to share with everyone. There was great anticipation when he called off the names and had everyone separate into two groups. No one knew which group would receive it and which one wouldn't until Steve joined one of them. He said in front of everyone that he would be getting it and would join the group that would also. As he moved toward the largest group, he could see the excitement on some people's faces. He then turned toward the smaller group and joined them. The room was silent on both sides. Only seventeen people would be receiving the gene therapy that would make them super human.

Ann appeared in front of all of them before they left the hangar.

"I need to explain to all of you why things are the way they are," she said. "The people that are compatible, she pointed to the small group, will receive great new abilities. The rest of you would ultimately turn into the worst things imaginable, I fear, and we simply cannot allow that."

The people on the airstrip had been split in their reactions after the news that most of them couldn't get the gene therapy. It didn't seem fair to some, and to others it made sense.

Simon was one of the people to get the therapy and didn't know what to think about it.

Ann could tell that he was troubled and took him aside to talk with him.

"You can say no," said Ann, "but know this. If you are injected, your body will heal itself and you will be young again and have all of your missing parts back. You will be able to access your entire brain power and believe me, you will enjoy a great new life."

Simon didn't know what to say to that. He just stared at Ann and thought for a minute.

"I'll let you know," said Simon. "Thank you."

Jake was still in a coma, after getting shot in the head while trying to save the people walking through the minefield; mines he helped put in the ground. His tissue sample had proven compatible and he would soon receive the gene therapy inoculation too.

Steve called for a meeting, but not everyone showed up and this was a concern. Some people had also stopped helping out around the compound. The little community that they had created was being torn apart since the arrival of the space shuttle and the people with the super human abilities.

A few of the men, ones who had come to live in the hangar from the city with Hans, wanted to leave. The group knew that they couldn't stop people from leaving, but the people that knew where the mines were or how security was set up were a risk and certain measures had to be taken to keep the compound safe. If the men left, they could tell others on the other side and the airstrip could be attacked.

The key members of the group got together without the others knowing to have a private meeting.

"If word spreads about the gene therapy then we will have chaos on our hands," said Gary.

"I agree," said Craig. "If these guys leave, then we may have to fight the whole city and I don't know if we have enough ammo for that."

"Let's not get to that point," said Steve. "We need to talk to Doug and Jim."

Nate was on the outside of the room keeping watch.

"Can you go and discreetly get Doug and Jim?" Craig asked Nate over the radio.

"On my way," said Nate. "You might want to post someone else out here while I'm gone."

"We will," said Craig, "thanks."

Nate was off to find the two men when he bumped into Sam.

"Hey man," said Sam. "Have you seen Steve? I need to talk to him about a few things."

"I think he's in his room," said Nate.

"No, I just came from there and he wasn't in it," said Sam.

"I don't know then," said Nate. "Talk to you later."

Nate was trying to leave so he could warn the others over the radio. As soon as Sam was gone he squelched his radio to alert them.

Doug and Jim were found over in the smaller hangar helping Chris put his jet back together. They had it almost fully assembled and it would be ready to fly within days.

"Hey guys," said Nate as he approached the jet.

"What are you up too?" asked Chris.

"I was wondering if I could borrow you three for a short time," said Nate.

"Do you need help with something?" asked Doug.

"I need to see if you guys are willing to help us with the dilemma we face with people wanting to leave," said Nate.

The men all stopped what they were doing and agreed to attend the private meeting. Sam was still out there, and Nate hoped to avoid him. They got to the room without incident and everything was explained to them.

"I think they should be able to leave if they want," said Doug. "We can help you defend this place if it comes to that."

"The problem is that they know where the mines are on the perimeter and how to spot them with night vision goggles," said Craig. "I don't think they should be allowed to leave because we know they want the inoculation and would do anything to get it."

"What do you suggest?" asked Jim. "Should we just execute them because we think they will do something?"

"The perimeter is very large for this amount of people to try to defend," said Craig. "We could be overrun in no time if attacked by a force that could enter wherever they wanted too."

"Why do they want to leave?" asked James. "Did anyone ask them that? We have more to offer them here than most places on the outside that we know of. I think Craig is right. They will leave and bring others back."

"We should give one of them the inoculation," said Ann as she walked in.

"How did you know we were here?" asked Craig.

"I could feel the tension in the air and could hear you as I got closer," said Ann.

"You know what will happen if we give them the gene therapy," said Doug.

"I know precisely," said Ann, "and that's why we should do it to show the others what will happen to them. We can take all the precautions necessary to ensure everyone's safety."

The rest of them agreed and the preparations were made to start the inoculations.

They all left the room and went their separate ways.

The next day, all of the people that had been told they would be receiving the gene therapy were asked to meet in the main hangar to discuss the next step.

"Simon and Jake will be the first ones to receive the shot," said Ann. "Once they have improved, we can start on the rest of you. Does anyone have any questions?"

"I do," said Sam as he walked in on the group. "When do we get our shot?"

"I was going to talk to the rest of you when I was done here," said Ann. "We have come up with a way around the problems and can start wide scale distribution soon."

"That's more like it," said Sam. "I'll let everyone else know. We don't need to bother you with a meeting."

With that, the astronauts made their preparations with Gary and Trevor assisting. Most of what they were doing was way beyond the doctor's comprehension.

"I graduated at the top of my class at Harvard Medical," said Gary, "and this stuff just doesn't make sense."

"It all will very soon," said Jill.

When they were ready, everyone waited in anticipation for the results, as the first two received the shot that would change their lives completely.

Simon walked by everyone that was waiting outside the medical center and said, "I'm ready to see if it will work."

Ann smiled at him. "You will not regret this one bit," she said.

Both Simon and Jake would be the first to get the inoculation. Some were still skeptical, but others were looking forward to it.

The time had come and everyone was ready in their own way. Trevor injected Simon and Gary injected Jake, after Ann gave them the syringes.

Within minutes of getting the shot, Jake woke up and looked around the room. The first thing he asked was, "Where's Lizzy?"

Gary was astounded. "Now just lay there Jake, we need to make sure that everything is okay before you go walking around."

Trevor took off the bandage that had been covering Jake's head wound as it healed. The wound had completely healed and his hair had grown back as well.

Simon was screaming.

"Wahoo!" said Simon.

"What's wrong?" asked Gary as he ran over to him.

"Everything's growing back," said Simon excitedly.

A camera had been set up in front of both men to document the effects of the shot. A reaction team had been assembled outside at Craig's request just in case they were needed. The team ran in and pointed their rifles at everyone when they heard Simon yelling.

"Put those guns down," said Gary.

Craig ordered everyone back out and went over to Simon.

"How do you feel buddy?" asked Craig.

"I feel wonderful," said Simon. "I have so many words to describe this, but I don't know which one to use first."

"You look much better, said Craig. I'm glad this all worked out for you. I wasn't going to let you die in that cave."

"Thanks Craig," said Simon as he looked into a mirror at his new face. His wrinkles were gone along with the bags under his eyes. He almost didn't recognize himself, but remembered that Ann said he would look young again, and did.

He had grown tired of looking at himself without a nose after he had lost it, and so much more, to frostbite. He had been wearing a facemask for months to hide it.

The two men would stay in the medical center under supervision for forty-eight hours to make sure that there were no side effects. The videos were taken out for everyone to watch in the hangar on a big-screen television. Ann didn't want anyone to bother them during the supervision time. There was excitement in the air as everyone watched the videos of Jake healing and waking up, and Simon growing his missing parts back and looking normal again.

Steve and the rest of the chosen few slowly received the treatment and quarantine time as well. The results were just as Ann and the others had explained. Craig was very happy to have the rest of his appendages back too after losing them to frostbite the winter before. Karen had to wait to get hers because she was still breast-feeding De Novo. No one knew what, if any problems he might have at such a young age. Everyone agreed that he could receive his once he matured. After receiving their inoculations, Gary and Trevor both read through the entire database on medicine and went to work on synthesizing antibiotics and other medicines in order to help heal the rest of the people that could not receive the new gift. They used Ann's research to help heal the sick faster, without actually giving them the advancement and putting the whole compound in danger. No one had even questioned why the astronauts were willing to share such a life changing ability, but once they received theirs, they understood fully. The men and women that were compatible and received the inoculation were changed forever and the people that were close to them could see the difference. They all looked younger and spoke with more authority. The elite group would make all things better for the whole.

Max, one of the men that had joined the group when they left the city for the airfield, was the one that was the most adamant about getting the injection. Sam was interested, but it was as if Max had the last word in most things with those men. No one other than the original four understood it. It would be Max that would be injected next. He was scheduled for the next morning and it would happen in a secure room that had been constructed just for the inoculation. A camera was set up so everyone could see a live feed on the big-screen television in the hangar. A large group had assembled with weapons outside the room as a precaution. Jim and Doug took Max into the room and had him lie down on a bed. He was then restrained and prepped for the shot. A few people could be heard wondering why he was put in restraints and soon found out why.

Jim injected Max and within seconds, he started convulsing and then went limp. He started thrashing wildly soon after and then calmed down again. He then raised his head and looked as if he was going to speak. Max started to scream very loud and started transforming. His arms started to get very large and broke through the restraints.

"He's mutating," said Doug.

Jim approached Max and was thrown across the room as he continued to break through the remaining restraints. Doug pulled out a sword that he had brought in the room and cut off Max's right arm and then cut off his head. The reaction team rushed into the room at the same time. All the people watching in the hangar couldn't believe what they had just seen.

Ann moved in front of the television. "Now do you understand why some of you can't get the gene therapy? I would love for all of you to share in these abilities that we possess, but it is just not in your genetic makeup to allow for this. I am truly sorry," said Ann, and walked away.

Steve walked over to everyone.

"This is why you can't join us in this," said Steve. "You are all welcome to stay and live with us. Nothing needs to change in that aspect."

"Everything has changed," said Bill. "You will always be looking at us as lower beings that can't do what you can."

"Please don't think that way," said Steve.

Bill walked away and Theresa followed him. The rest of the people just walked away from Steve.

Craig walked up to Steve. "You can't win them all buddy," he said.

"Those are my friends... our friends," said Steve. "We will continue on with Ann's work and find a way."

Chapter Ten: Evolution

Chris's jet was now completely reassembled. With the extra help from Jim and Doug, the job went much faster and the added intelligence from the gene therapy made it so those two didn't second-guessed their work. It was all done right the first time and more efficiently.

The jet was ready for its test flight. This might prompt another attack from the group that had attempted entry onto the airfield not too long ago, but they would be ready if it happened.

Jake was fully recovered and back in the saddle. The woman and child that he had gone to save the day he was shot were very happy to see him.

"Lizzy kept my spirit alive," said Jake as they sat and talked.

"We are in your debt, if you need anything," said Nicole as she grabbed Jake's hand and held it.

"Thank you," said Jake. He got up and shook Nicole's hand and hugged Lizzy.

Many of the men got together and the jet was rolled out of the hangar, pulled by a Hummer. Chris and Doug would take it up for a test flight. They both had parachutes on just in case. Everyone came out to watch. The jet started up and within minutes was rolling down the runway to get into position for takeoff. James was in the control tower with a radio he had rigged up for the take-off and landing coordination. There was very little wind that day and James saw nothing from the tower that might stop them from taking off, so he gave Chris the go-ahead.

The jet powered up and roared down the runway. It took off with ease and began climbing. The roar of the engines from a plane or jet was something that no one had heard in years and was exciting to some. The two men were going to put it through its paces to make sure it worked well to go on a long distance trip.

While the jet was gone, some of the people sat around and talked and others went back to work.

Almost an hour later, they announced that they were on final approach. James said that all was clear and they could land. The jet came in and made a perfect touchdown. Many of the people were anxious to hear from Chris and Doug what the ground looked like from the air.

Sam walked up to Steve and Craig as everyone waited for the jet to come to a stop outside the hangar.

"I want to apologize for the way I acted before," said Sam. "Max was, you could say, our leader and we listened to him. The other guys and I want to stay and know we are better off here with you and know that this community needs us too. We appreciate all that we have and couldn't be happier with all of our new friends. You have our support back and thank you for opening our eyes to the horror that we could have experienced."

Steve and Craig accepted his apology and went over to meet Chris and Doug.

After the men and women talked for a while, the jet was rolled back into the hangar for preparation for going to Texas.

Auxiliary fuel tanks were mounted under the wings and everything was doubled checked for the following day's flight.

After the flight, Craig assembled teams to check the perimeter to make sure that all was still good for the security of the compound, since there was more activity now. Each team checked their area and met back at the hangar to discuss a plan for if they were attacked. Craig and Jake would be going with Chris to Texas, so Joe was in charge of the security and took control of the plan.

The next morning, the three men left in the jet. The old silo was supposed to be used for experiments while Chris was gone, and the others would stay on the surface; but the plan for further experimentation was called off after Max had been given the inoculation and mutated. There was no reason to put everyone in danger. The gene altering drug inoculation made everyone who had it so much better all by itself, so why try to go further when you already had perfection, most asked?

Only Chris, Ben and Sherri had been able to get the gene therapy. Ben's wife had hoped to get it too so she could share that life with him. Chris' daughters were not old enough yet and could get it in a few years. The people that couldn't get it were disappointed, but also knew that they were better off living their lives out with their friends and families.

The trip to Texas would take less than three hours. Once they got there, they would have to fly low and slow to get a good look at the airstrip, to see if they could land. The men were prepared for almost any contingency.

The day on the airfield was another one spent preparing for winter. They expected to have a pretty mild one, being further south, but they all wanted to be prepared just in case.

The nights were growing colder and this one was no exception. Clouds were approaching and it was getting darker out. Around 1 a.m. it started to rain and the men in the tower on watch were glad they were indoors.

A flare was launched up into the air just after 2 a.m., followed by explosions on the south end of the airstrip. The reaction team was assembled and two Hummers went to investigate. Joe told the two men in the tower to stay there and keep watching the whole perimeter. When the Hummers reached the end of the airstrip, machine gun fire riddled them. The turret gunners fired back in small bursts in the direction of the muzzle flashes.

After about thirty seconds, the men with radios heard, "Cease fire!" Joe was yelling on the radio over the gunfire. "Tower, give me a sit rep. Do you see anything on the rest of the perimeter?"

"I see nothing from here," said Stan, a very muscular man from Sam's group.

"Wait, here we go," said Bill. "I see multiple human figures running toward the main hangar."

"Sound the alarm!" said Joe. "Second team, I want Hummers to engage the threat coming toward you. Do not move too far away from the hangar"

The other two Hummers pulled out of the hangar and moved toward the hostiles. A firefight ensued. The machine guns on the southern end opened up again on the two Hummers down there.

"It's a coordinated attack!" yelled Joe. "Tower, I want you to call out targets that are not already being engaged. They're up to something."

"You got it," said Bill.

They were being attacked on two sides now, and then the unexpected happened.

"I see vehicles moving through the mine field and about to... They just crashed through the front gate," said Stan.

"Team two, I want one Hummer to move to the front gate," said Joe. "I'm on my way."

Joe instructed the other Hummer to stay where it was and not let anyone past them. *How could that vehicle have made it through the minefield?* he wondered. Everyone was to fight from the vehicles and not to engage on foot. This would give them the advantage over their attackers because of the armor on the vehicles. They were now being engaged from three sides, and Joe hoped that was all. With only a small number of men in the hangars protecting everything and everyone else, the teams needed to keep the attackers away from them.

The two Hummers rolled up on the front gate to engage the vehicles that had come through. The .50 cal's ripped the trucks up and they caught fire after the fuel tanks were hit.

The machine guns in the turrets were getting a workout and getting hot. Some were on five reloads by now and Joe was getting concerned. The rain was helping cool them off, but they couldn't keep a sustained firefight going. The guns could seize up or they could just run out of ammo.

"All Hummers make your way back here," said Joe. "We will make a smaller area to defend by putting the Hummers in a 180 around the hangars. We can fill in the gaps with men on the ground. Only the men with the gene therapy are to exit the vehicles and proceed on foot."

Hans and Sam went to get sniper rifles from the armory and went up into the control tower to engage targets that were further out in hopes of either slowing them down for the guys on the ground or stopping the attack completely. They started engaging targets firing machine guns and then others in turn.

Stan and Bill kept calling out targets to the Hummer teams. The attackers just kept coming. The gunfire slowed down for the remainder of the morning and the rain stopped as daylight slowly emerged on the horizon. Men with scopes engaged the further targets along with Hans and Sam.

Dozens of bodies lay all over the airstrip. The vehicles that had come through the front gate were still smoldering. No one was alive that they could see. Bill and Stan gave the all clear after awhile and Hans confirmed it. They would still be cautious by remaining on over watch, but it appeared to be over.

After the sun came up, Joe told the rest of the men in the hangars to come out and help with the body and weapons collection. The perimeter would have to be reestablished after they had broken through. Snipers in the tower and on upper levels of the hangars provided over watch while this happened.

No one in the compound had died. Two men had been shot and taken to the medical center. Joe had been shot five times and as he healed, the bullets that hadn't gone all the way through him had come back out and fell onto the ground. He picked them up and put them in his pocket.

The cleanup continued and the men only took breaks to eat. Joe wanted the perimeter back to one hundred percent before nightfall. The ability to see further and react faster had really helped them win the fight. Joe and some of the others with the gene had been shot; they couldn't dodge all the bullets, but did a great job nonetheless.

Meanwhile, over the skies of Texas the day before, the men in the jet were moving in for a closer look at the landing strip. Chris slowed the jet down so they could see better.

"I see a few trees lying on a few parts of the runway," said Chris as they got closer.

"I know what to do," said Craig. "Take us back up to ten thousand feet and we'll radio you when it's all clear."

The jet circled over the area and climbed. Once it reached ten thousand feet, Craig opened the door and he and Jake jumped. The two men were supposed to open their parachutes as soon as they exited the jet, but Craig was having problems with his. He finally got it to open at about five thousand feet. The parachute almost instantly turned into a streamer.

Craig pulled on the steering toggles to try to open it up, but this had no effect so he broke away from his parachute at around five hundred feet. He was on his way to earth at over one hundred miles an hour. Craig hit the ground and it looked like a bomb had exploded. There was a large cloud of dust as Jake glided over to him.

Once Jake could see through the cloud, he could tell that Craig was not moving and was lying flat on his stomach. His right arm was twisted and so was his left leg. There was blood pouring out of his body in some places. Jake rolled him over and saw a broken man in front of him. Craig was starting to heal already and Jake just stood there and watched. In a few minutes, Craig started breathing again and slowly stood up.

"Man that hurt," said Craig as he shook his head. "We had better get going."

The two men made their way to the airstrip and took off their gear. Craig's tactical gear and weapons were almost worthless now after the fall and everything was stained with blood. They started moving trees and broken branches. An hour later, Chris was ready to land the jet. He made one more pass just to make sure he liked what he saw and finally put it down. He moved up toward the hangar and shut the aircraft down.

"Let's get inside and see what they left us," said Chris. "How was the landing Craig?"

Chris was smiling, but Craig didn't think it was funny.

"If I hadn't packed my own parachute, I would think that you did," said Craig.

The men went into the hangar and saw that people had been living in it. They brought their weapons up, turned on weapon lights and began to search the building. They found it to be empty except for a couple of ripped up tents and trash everywhere, so Chris led them to the entrance to the bunker. Chris pushed on the wall in a few different areas and this opened a door that was part of the wall. He went in and turned on the lights. Jake stayed topside for the time being in case someone came back.

Chris led Craig down into the bunker as if he had been there the whole time. The place was brand new and full of many items that would be useful to the group back in Idaho.

"It would be nice to have a bigger aircraft to take more back," said Craig. "What do you want to take this trip?"

"We need some electronics and we should take as much food as we can too," said Chris.

The two men packed the totes up the stairs and Jake stacked them up. Bags were brought up as well. The plastic totes would fill the aircraft up very fast, so to fill the small areas, items were put in bags.

The bunker was sealed back up when they got all they could into the jet. They all got back in, took off and headed toward another location.

"Why aren't we headed back home?" asked Jake.

"I want to fly over the old west coast and see what it looks like," said Chris.

The detour would take them four hours out of their way and they wouldn't get back to their airstrip in Idaho until the following morning.

They had plenty of fuel after Chris refueled in Texas.

The men flew at ten to fifteen thousand feet most of the way to get a better view. The devastation they saw in most cities was unimaginable. Chris had finally seen enough and headed back home. The men didn't talk much on the way back, so Chris put music on.

A few hours later, the jet was fifty miles out and Chris couldn't contact anyone on the ground. He decided to do a flyby to look at the airstrip. As the jet flew overhead low and slow, they could see that the compound had been attacked. The men on the ground were still cleaning up. They were all looking up as the jet flew by. Chris decided to do some recon of the area until they could land.

James saw them fly by and finally contacted them on the radio to explain everything.

"Just let us know when we can land," said Chris. "We're pretty cramped up here."

"I will call you just as soon as we get an area cleared," said James.

The jet was finally able to land and when it rolled up to the hangar, everyone that wasn't cleaning up or checking the perimeter came to help them unload.

"How was the trip?" asked Doug.

"I'm glad you guys gave us these cool new abilities," said Craig, "or I wouldn't be here right now."

Doug looked at him with a blank look on his face as he realized all of his clothing and gear was torn and bloody.

"I'll explain later brother," said Craig.

The jet was pushed back into its hangar and as the day came to an end, everyone felt good about what had been accomplished. They still didn't know precisely why they were being attacked, but knew it had something to do with what they had and what the others wanted.

It had only been a short time, but much had happened. Each group told their story about what they had gone through in the last two days. Everyone was laughing at Craig's story about his free fall with a broken parachute.

"It's not funny," he said with a smile.

As the days passed, the people that had received the gene therapy realized more about their new abilities and started to see their full potential.

Chapter Eleven: Construction

Winter was coming, but a bad one was not anticipated, being further south. Ann's baby bump was starting to show and Karen offered to help her with anything she needed. Bill and Theresa had let their relationship be known and it seemed like everyone was getting comfortable again. No more attempts had been made at the compound. The attackers from the city had lost a large number of their men, weapons and ammo while trying to get in the last time, so hopefully they realized that it wasn't worth it to try again. A small recon element had gone into town to gather information. Chris and some of the other men had been making more trips to retrieve supplies from the Texas bunker. They decided to take a break for a few days and help out around the compound.

Doug had been working and making a lot of noise in the empty hangar he had asked to use. He wouldn't tell anyone what he was working on except that it would be very beneficial to everyone. Weeks went by and after lunch one day, he asked if anyone was interested. He invited them to come and see what he had been working on.

Many in the group were very curious, so about two-dozen people showed up to see. Doug asked everyone to stand out of the way. Nate was anxious, and took off a cover anyway. They could see what looked like a tube with wires attached to it, and another thing that almost resembled a rifle.

"Ok, so what are they?" asked someone in the crowd.

"An engine and a weapon," said Nate with a proud smile on his face.

"Ok, so give us a rundown," said Chris.

"This engine is based on ion pulse technology, just as this rifle is," said Doug.

"So, how does it work?" asked Sam.

"The particles push very hard against each other much like two very strong magnets. The harder they push the more energy is produced, and they need a regulator like this gadget so they don't go ballistic."

"You mean explode," asked Steve.

"Yes," said Doug, "and it would be a very large explosion and be devastating." Doug demonstrated the engine for everyone. He started it up and as he cranked up the repulsion, the engine began to float.

"How is it floating?" asked Karen.

"The direction of the repulsion is harnessed and a command is given with these controls."

"That is amazing," said Bill.

Some of them understood what was being said, others still had no idea what it all meant. The basics of gun and engine were easy enough, but the details were what they didn't understand.

"Can we try the rifle now?" asked Hans.

"Yes we can," said Doug. "I figured that it would get the most attention."

Targets were set up and hearing and eye protection were handed out. Hans was the first to try it. He aimed through the scope, which was just a tube with no cross hairs, and fired it. In an instant, the target was destroyed. "Incredible, there is no recoil and that man-sized target is gone. You have to tell us how this works, and where is the magazine? What kinds of projectiles are fired from it?" asked Hans.

"This weapon is very different from your encased projectile weapons you're used to," said Doug. "A block of titanium is loaded into this chamber and then it is slowly shaved off as the weapon is fired. With the repulsion so rapid, each piece is fired at approximately eight thousand feet per second and has an impact force of more than 40,000 foot pounds of kinetic energy. Nothing on earth would be able to survive one blast from this weapon."

"Why are you building such powerful weapons?" asked Nicole. "Or better yet, why are you building weapons?"

Everyone looked over at her and then back at Doug.

"We need to defend ourselves and the better the weapons, the less we will have to use them," said Doug.

"I am just tired of all the killing," said Nicole.

"I think we all are," said Steve. "Many of us went underground to survive the bombs and have been fighting for our lives ever since we came back to the surface. I would like to live in a peaceful world and so would everyone else here I would hope."

The excitement was over and everyone left except for Steve.

"I would like to get your help with my project," said Doug. "In fact, I would like many of you to help. We need to start construction as soon as possible."

The group that had been inoculated with the gene therapy which essentially made them super human, started speaking ancient Latin to one another. It was as if they had their own language. Even someone that spoke Latin would have a hard time understanding the dialect. Some of the others didn't like that this small group was talking amongst themselves in a language no one else could under-stand. They started writing in a strange language too. It turned out to be Latin also. With the ability to access all of their brain, they could learn anything they wanted or needed in a very short time and were able to retain all of it. They were the next evolution of humankind, some thought.

Once a plan was devised, materials were brought in from the outside by the truckload and taken to the han-gar that Doug was working in. Many of the others were there helping him also. A small power plant was con-structed before the first phase could start. The power that would be needed would be substantial. The plant was built using the same technology that Doug used to make the weapon and the engine. They could regulate the output and run everything in the compound as well as the construction area. It was a clean energy and gen-erated much more than the windmill and solar panels.

A smelting plant had been built also and material was being made for constructing something.

No one knew what they were building at first, but it was being put together very fast. More of the group volunteered to help, mostly out of curiosity, but also to help their friends.

In a few months, the shape of a ship could be seen in the project. It was a strange looking ship, and it had everyone asking more questions.

The material that was brought in and then fabricated after being melted down was being made into titanium alloy and high-strength carbon steel. The strongest and lightest metal was used for the skin, the outer hull of the ship. The carbon steel was used for the inner hull. Due to its high melting point of 2,800 degrees Fahrenheit it could protect the ship from many things. The titanium had a low melting point of around 800 degrees Fahrenheit, but it's resistance to corrosion and nonmagnetic properties made it perfect for the outside. Both types of steel had been chosen for different reasons. With the abilities that the craft would have, it would not need high temperature tiles to absorb heat. The new engines would slow the velocity to a point that the ship would not look like a fireball streaking across the sky, like the space shuttle on re-entry. The speed and maneuverability would be impressive as well.

Doug and Chris were busy working on the engines. James and Steve were putting in electrical and computer systems, many of which came from the space shuttle. Everyone else was busy with the fabricating. It was a big job and about forty people were involved.

Simon only came to help when he was done with his work with the animals. The first batch was maturing nicely and was being taken care of by some of the women and children under Susan's supervision. She had helped Simon from the beginning and continued to be very handy. One of the smaller hangars had been converted to house the animals and their food. They would soon be old enough to be eaten, reproduce and provide milk for the group. The chickens had started to produce eggs and everyone was enjoying them.

"What kind of plane is this?" Stan asked Doug one day.

"Interstellar," said Doug, and then walked away.

"I don't get it," said Stan.

"Star ship," said Steve.

"You're telling me that we're building a spaceship?" asked Stan.

"Well, it's more like an everywhere ship," said Jim. "We will be able to fly through the air, in space and even go underwater."

"Will all of us be able to go?" asked Stan.

"Only if you stop talking and help," said Craig as he walked by.

They all continued to work, until Karen came in with some bad news, and everyone stopped.

"Bill has just died," said Karen, "and Margret is acting strange."

The workday was close to its end, so everyone stopped where they were and went to help if they could.

"She's in shock," said Gary as he examined Margret and Bill. "You're right, Bill is dead."

"We should get them both into the medical facility," said Trevor.

Steve whispered something in Margret's ear and she let go of Bill and went with him to get checked out.

"We will need to bury him quickly," Gary told Karen. "We have no refrigeration big enough to store him like a morgue would."

A burial detail was put together in an area designated by Steve on the far southern end of the airstrip. He had to be buried far enough away from the water source; he would be the first of many as time went by. This would be the first person lost to the group in what seemed like a long time. Bill was a very fun and loving man. Margret was still in shock and Gary didn't see her lasting much longer. The two had been together for so many years that one couldn't live without the other. James offered to learn the system that Bill and Margret had put in place for the water supply, so he could maintain it.

The funeral was planned for the next morning. Work on the ship would be postponed for a short time. This unfortunate circumstance gave them all some time to rest. It made everyone stop to appreciate and enjoy each other.

Steve was talking to De Novo on the bed in their room. Karen entered and walked over to them.

"Do you know what the purpose of this ship is that Doug is so adamant about building?" asked Karen.

"It will benefit all of us," said Steve.

"How will it benefit us?" asked Karen.

"He hasn't told us yet," said Steve.

"I was just wondering, is it for transportation, a war ship, what?" asked Karen.

"We will find out soon," said Steve.

"You've been right every step of the way," said Karen. "I will continue to stand by you."

The three of them lay on the bed and fell asleep.

The next morning, everyone got ready for the funeral. Ray and Joe walked in with a nice casket for Bill.

"Where did you get that?" asked Trevor as the men brought it into the medical center.

"We were up all night building it," said Ray.

They could all smell the fresh stain on the wood.

"Margret will be very happy with you two," said Gary.

Bill was placed in the casket and taken into the hangar for a small service. Steve got up and spoke about the man Bill was and how he and Margret had been married for almost fifty years.

After the service, Bill's casket was placed on top of his drill truck and everyone made their way to the makeshift cemetery. Only a few people had to walk, most rode on the truck or in the Hummers.

Bill was laid to rest and everyone slowly got back to their duties or back to the ship. Two days later, Margret was found dead in her bed. She had passed in her sleep. She too was given a nice burial.

Construction on the new ship continued through the winter. The space shuttle was more or less gutted in order to get the new ship operational. The shape looked circular from the front, but from up above it looked like a V. The ship didn't look very aero dynamic, but it didn't need to be because of the maneuvering thrusters it had. Doug explained that it would be able to take off like the old Harrier and hover. It could also change directions without a wide turn. Even at great speeds, it wouldn't be torn apart.

"Won't the inertia rip the ship apart, without slowing down or taking a wide turn instead?" asked Bill as Doug explained everything.

"The maneuvering thrusters will compensate for the G-forces combined with speed," said Doug. "With the level of technology that we are incorporating here, it will be like a helicopter was in the early nineteen hundreds. Revolutionary is the best word to describe this ship," said Doug.

Everyone was excited to fly in the new ship. It was not only large enough for everyone in the compound to fit in at once, but if what Doug said was true then they might be going into space too. Besides the astronauts, Chris was the only other one that had gone into outer space.

The men continued to bring in materials for the project. Sometimes they would tell about the bandits that tried to ambush them and the vehicles. The attacks were all extinguished quickly. With most of the men able to withstand being shot many times, and heal very quickly, they were no match for anyone else. They didn't go looking for a fight, but won every engagement that was presented to them.

The holidays were in full swing this year and with the availability of animals, the meals were much better. No turkey was available for Thanksgiving, but chicken was. Fresh vegetables from Nancy's garden in the loft made the meals more enjoyable too. Not all the animals were ready for consumption, but the ones that were made great meals. Simon was working on a second batch while the first ones were maturing.

"We can't have enough food," said Simon while working with Susan.

Christmas was just a festival. The idea of gifts was a thing of the past with this group. Most people would rather just have a nice meal and enjoy everyone's company.

The ship was completed by early spring and everyone involved anticipated its launch.

Doug said the ship was ready one sunny morning and preparations were made to tow it out of the hangar. Three Hummers had to pull the large ship out with heavy tow straps. As the ship was being towed out onto the airstrip, Doug was going through the preflight with the men and woman onboard and checking all of the operating systems. The ship was towed to the middle of the small airstrip. The Hummers would stop and the tow straps would be taken off. There were five people on board to operate all the required systems. The maiden voyage was going to be just a short trip to test everything.

Once they came to a stop, the tow straps were taken off, Hummers moved out of the way and Doug started the engines. Besides a little dust being kicked up, there was very little sound or disturbance. Chris started going through each maneuvering thruster one at a time as they were being verified on the outside.

All of the maneuvering thrusters were tested, firing small bursts. A few hatches opened up and the weapons came out into view and then were retracted. The whole time this was going on, three other men were walking around the outside talking on radios to Jill and the others inside.

All the systems were in the green, so Doug had everyone sit down for takeoff.

The three men on the outside moved out of the way and the ship started to hover and rotate left to right. A viewing window could be seen as the skin on the outer hull slid into itself. Everyone could see Doug and Chris at the controls and the others walking around to take their seats at their stations. The front window was just one of many. This one was for the pilot and navigator. There were more windows on the sides of the ship too. The ship hovered and rose to about one hundred feet and then took off with great speed. There was still very little sound as all of this happened, and when it vanished with great velocity, everyone was shocked.

They rose very quickly and the people on board continued to check their designated areas of the ship. Doug took it up to fifty thousand feet in under a minute. The onboard computers quickly compensated for the change in atmosphere and mixed the right ratio of air for the group on board. Since they were all buckled into their chairs, when Doug started to perform maneuvers the G forces had no effect on them. The design of the ship, and the computers compensating for every possible action, made flying at great speed and maneuverability very easy.

Doug brought the ship down for a flyby of the airstrip where everyone was watching. He then brought it to a stop and hovered right in front of the group. Legs were then extended from the belly and the ship came to a complete stop on the airstrip. Steve lowered the ramp and they all came out. There were smiles and cheering from most everyone on the ground.

Many people wanted to go for a ride. Doug told them all that they would get a chance to go on trips.

"We are entering a new era in human existence," said Steve, "and all of you can be a part of it. We will need to gather much more material and we will need more people to accomplish our next goal."

"What do you plan to do next?" asked Sam.

"We will be building more ships that will be much larger than this one," said Doug.

The people in the crowd look surprised, but they knew that they were on the best side of the fence.

The ship was flown inside the hangar. The legs were extended and it was parked.

There were plans already being drawn up to build larger ships. These ships would be able to hold much more of everything. They would be built so that they would be able to fit together and form a much larger ship too, according to the drawings. This ship, once assembled, would be able to go much faster with the multiple engines pushing it. They would be able to match speeds and attach while in flight as well as when they were hovering just above the ground.

Chapter Twelve:Novus Ordo Seclorum (A New Order of the Ages)

Most of the people in the group were wondering and asking questions about more and larger ships. Why they were needed and why so many.

Doug called a meeting for everyone to hear his plan.

"I want to thank all of you for your tireless efforts in building our scout ship," said Doug. "As you all know, we have plans for making more and larger ships that will do so much more than this one you have helped construct. You all right here, are a part of the next step in our evolution as a species. We will need approximately one hundred more people to help with the construction that is about to start. We will first need to build housing for them. Ray will be in charge of this phase and then James and Steve will take on the second phase of ship construction. Does anyone have any questions?" asked Doug.

"How are we going to feed these one hundred new people?" asked Sherri. "We have fifty people right now and are just barely making it."

"Simon is working on that issue already and has said that we will be just fine," said Doug.

The warmer weather that was upon the valley, made the overall mood better for most of the group. No one wanted to continue to work as hard as they had been, but this was a 'dog-eat- dog' world now and the airstrip compound was the best place to be for most of them. They had food, shelter and clean water. This was so much more than most of the people that they had encountered so far since leaving their sanctuaries or coming to live on the airfield.

The new ship was called the 'Virtus' which means strength, power through courage and bravery. It transported working groups to Chris's various bunkers around the country that he had built as contingencies. He didn't know where he and his family would be at the time that they might need shelter, so he had many built. Most of them were still intact. He had them built miles away from the cities so they wouldn't be destroyed if something happened.

The groups of people were different every time the workers left, in order to let everyone get a chance to help and experience the new ship.

New people started arriving by the dozens. Many of them had military backgrounds like AJ, a tall blond haired man that had been a fighter pilot. They were picked by Craig and his team in order to best help with the construction of the ships, given their fields of expertise. They were offered food, shelter and protection in exchange for their part in the construction. Craig had warned all of them before they were taken in that there would be consequences for any lawlessness that came from them. Some of the people brought families, but most were your basic refugee that had lost more than they cared to talk about. Everyone would have a place in the compound, from the men to the women and children. A new world was being constructed from the remnants of the old one. This was the beginning of a future that they all could look forward to. Ray reported that raw materials were getting harder to find in the local area and that resistance by marauders was increasing. The main group got together to discuss the problems and find solutions.

"We can take the incoming fire and survive, but the other workers that we need that don't have the advances we do are being wounded or killed," said Jake.

"Can anyone think of a way that we can protect people better and accomplish the mission?" asked Craig.

"We are just about done getting supplies," said Doug. "The ship can be used for transporting materials for constructing the new ships."

"We need body armor," said Steve. "I will design a prototype and we can test it."

"Problems solved," said Jim.

They all got back to their duties and the new plans were implemented.

After the rest of the supplies had been recovered from the bunkers that Chris had built, the ship was flown over to the bunkers that Steve's group had constructed in Montana. The area and bunkers had been left untouched and the rest of the supplies there were brought back. The ship was available to start getting raw materials to fabricate more parts for the new ships. Six ships were planned for, and no one knew yet how long it would take. The first smaller one took about six months with forty-five people working on it. Now that that ship was ferrying supplies, it made the process faster and many more people were building the necessary components. They would have a better idea when the first one could be done. A small group of men and women that Craig had found were chosen because of their electronics, or computer backgrounds. These people were building the necessary components for the new ships' navigation and control systems based on Doug's designs. It was complicated for some, but luckily others were able to get the gene therapy.

Steve meanwhile had enlisted James to help him with the body armor. The two men started with design ideas but nothing they came up with would cover all vital parts and allow the men to move enough to do the work they would need to do.

"What about a suit?" asked Karen.

Karen had been standing there watching the two men work for about forty-five minutes one day and had seen what they were trying to do.

Steve and James looked at each other in amazement.

"Now why didn't we think of that?" asked James, as he looked at Karen and then back at Steve.

"Because you were too busy focusing on just certain parts," said Karen.

Karen walked up to the men and took the marker from James. She went to the board and started drawing.

"You can make a slender suit that has pliable material in all the movable parts of the body. If you use thin Titanium with the same technology as the ships with repulsion, then the men inside of them would be invincible and still be able to move around with ease," said Karen.

"What kind of material would we use for the pliable parts of the suit?" asked Steve.

"You can use Kevlar," said Doug as he walked into the room. "Someone has been paying attention. Karen will be a great addition to the group once she is inoculated. I can bring you one of the suits that we used outside of the space shuttle," said Doug. "It should aid you in perfecting your design of a suit that will work for us."

Karen kissed Steve on the cheek and walked away smiling, with De Novo in his backpack. Once Steve and James got the suit that Doug told them about in the shuttle, they went to work. They started with taking the space suit completely apart so they could see everything that they would need to do to make theirs more conformed to the human body, lighter, more maneuverable and still able to function like the one they had in front of them. It would be built as if it was going to be in space, and it might one day. The men knew that they would need more material and they knew where they could find it. They located the nearest military base on a map and told Doug that the next trip out with the ship would have two more passengers and a slight detour.

When the ship was ready to leave, Steve and James walked up the ramp. The men on board looked a little taken aback at the men dressed in full combat gear. They had security as they scavenged for metal, but nobody ever had that much gear on.

The Virtus took off as the ramp was being raised and sealed. Steve walked to the flight deck to give Doug the coordinates of the army base that he and James needed to be dropped off at. The ship was at the base in no time at all with its great speed. Doug flew low and slow around the whole area for reconnaissance before putting it down to let Steve and James out. The base was deserted and much of it was destroyed.

"Good luck guys," Doug said to the men over the radio as they walked to the rear of the ship. Doug lowered the ramp and they got out. They walked toward one of the only structures left standing to search it for what they needed.

"What are the odds of us finding any Kevlar?" James asked Steve.

"I'm not quite sure," said Steve as they entered the building.

"We've found the armory," said James. "The hardened walls must have protected it better than the others."

The men searched the armory. The weapons that they were sure were stored inside had been gone for some time. The other side of the building looked like a supply warehouse. They searched room to room but not much was left.

"I found something," said Steve.

James walked over to see what it was and saw a pile of flak jackets and helmets.

"These must have been too heavy for the looters to want to carry," said James.

"What do you think about those odds James?" asked Steve.

The two men smiled and began to take the items that they thought would work best out to the area where Doug had dropped them off.

An hour later, they were sitting on a pile of Kevlar vests that would help them make their suits. The Virtus flew overhead and came back to land. A few men came out of the ship to help Steve and James load their plunder. The entire ship was full of scrap metal for use in constructing the new ships.

With the Virtus shuttling material to the construction site, the new ship was being built at a record pace. Steve and James were putting the first suit together pretty fast too. Karen was called in to help figure out how the suit would be worn.

"There will have to be two pieces," said Karen. "The upper torso and the lower will have to attach together with overlapping layers hanging from the top."

A prototype was almost finished. The helmet was the last piece to build. The eye piece was going to be the difficult part. They would need high strength Lexan for its scratch proof, bullet resistant, and UV resistant properties, but didn't know where they would find it.

"The astronaut's helmets," said James all of a sudden. "They already have the material that we need."

"We can also add a camera in the helmet that can display on a heads-up display if the eyepiece needs to be closed," said Steve.

"Yes," said James. "The helmet can be tied into the environmental system of the suit I have been working on."

The two men continued to bounce ideas off of each other.

"My work here is done," said Karen as she walked out of the room.

By the end of the summer, the new ship, which was to be called the 'Intrepidus' meaning 'fearless' in Latin, was almost complete. Steve and James were ready to test their new full-body armored suit. Steve was happy with the test that had been done with no one in it, so he volunteered to be the first human test subject with the suit on.

He walked out of the room with James close behind him. A few people were laughing and quickly stopped when Steve stopped and looked at them. He looked menacing and was much taller in the suit. Steve walked out to the shooting range that had been built the year before for the live fire testing. Work stopped all around the compound just for the test. A Hummer had been brought out to fire a .50 cal at Steve and various other weapons were assembled. For safety purposes, everyone was in the main hangar watching on the big screen. Jake was filming the whole thing from the Hummer.

Steve was going to test his weapon first. A small cannon came out of Steve's right forearm and he pointed it at a target down range. The weapon was tied into the HUD and the targeting system, so all he had to do was point in the direction of the target. He started firing and completely destroyed the man-sized target that had been set up. He then walked down to the berm so he could be fired upon. He radioed that he was ready and Craig fired an M4 at him. The bullets could be seen hitting the ground all around him as they were deflected away from the suit. Joe picked up an M60 and had the same effect when he fired it full auto at Steve. Next was the .50 cal with Ray in the turret. Steve told Ray he was ready. Ray started shooting with the machinegun. The weapon thumped away and Steve moved his cover down over his eyes and raised his left arm. A small Titanium shield popped up from his left forearm and opened up to aid in the deflection of the large bullets. He moved his shield to the left as Ray started firing and the bullets deflected to a target that he had set up earlier and destroyed it. The people watching in the hangar were going wild.

The shooting stopped and Steve approached the camera to show everyone that he was just fine. The suit had performed just like he and James had designed it. The suit had defensive and offensive capabilities and should work as a space suit as well. The next test would have to be underwater to make sure that everything had been sealed correctly.

The demonstration was so impressive that James and Steve were asked by their small group to continue on with making more suits.

As fall approached, a classroom was set up for the kids. A few of the older ones didn't want to go to school, but Jillian lectured them on how the remaining humans on the planet had to rebuild their civilization and to do that, they would need knowledge. The kids listened to her reasoning and relented.

Simon's farm animals were doing great and they were all reproducing at this point. There was plenty of food for the small community that had been created on the airstrip and they all seemed happy.

One evening just before dark while most people were going to bed, a radio call prompted many of them to consolidate into the large hangar. A guard in the tower had spotted a woman walking toward the main gate. She was acting erratically and was just barely missing the mines on her way in. A reaction team got in a Hummer and sped off toward the gate. When they got there, four men got out while Stan stayed in the turret seat. Craig approached the gate and told the woman not to move. He unlocked the gate and caught the woman as she fell. Craig immediately felt strange. He turned around and said, "Stay where you are!" to the others as they approached. "Gary, this is Craig, over."

"This is Gary, go ahead."

"Gary, I think we have a situation here," said Craig. "Please bring me a cocktail."

"On my way Craig," said Gary.

Another Hummer raced toward the main gate. When it got there, Gary got out and approached Craig.

"What does she have?" asked Gary.

"I don't know doc," said Craig, "but I don't feel real good."

"Defense team standby," said Gary as he felt the effects too.

Gary gave the woman an inoculation and she went limp in Craig's arms. The two men started feeling better and the woman started to wake up.

"What's your name?" asked Gary.

"Samantha," said the woman. "Where am I?"

"Incoming!" yelled Joe, as bullets started whizzing by and hitting the men and vehicles.

"Back to the Hummers," said Craig as he carried Samantha. "Doug, we need the ship, now," said Craig over the radio.

Within a minute, the Virtus was airborne and hovering above the Hummers. The ion pulse cannons started to pound the building in front of the airstrip and the small hills too.

"Give me thermal on the HUD," said Doug.

The heads-up display on the flight deck turned grey and showed a few remaining combatants in the area.

"Light them up," Doug said to Hans, who was at the gunner's console.

A few more bursts fired and that was it, nothing else was moving down below.

"You're all clear ground team," said Doug as the ship flew back to the hangar.

The men got back into the Hummers and took Samantha to the medical center to get checked out.

When they got back, Ann was there to meet them.

"That was reckless doctor," said Ann. "What if she had the wrong genetic makeup? You could have killed many people. Ann stopped and stared at Samantha then said, "She was poisoned with a large dose of radiation. She is sorry she came to hurt us, but they made her."

"You're right Ann," said Gary, "and it won't happen again."

Samantha was placed in an observation room and guarded while everyone else got together for a meeting.

"I'm taking the gene therapy and I will decide who gets inoculated from now on," said Ann.

"You don't know what it was like out there," said Craig. "I really thought that I was dying and Gary was just trying to help."

"I just wanted to save my friend," said Gary, "and I calculated the odds. I had the security team standing by to terminate if needed."

"The only way that she would have died would have been to have her head cut off," said Jim. "It was, however, an extreme situation and one that Gary has learned from."

"Still," said Ann. "The gene therapy will stay with me for now. I appreciate the compassion you have for one another and the will to survive. We can't just hand this out to anyone that we encounter. We were all chosen for a yet unrevealed reason."

"What do you mean?" asked James. "You designed the gene therapy aboard the space station is what you told all of us when you came here."

"Is there something we need to know?" asked Chris.

"All will be revealed at the appropriate time," said Ann. "That is all that I know."

Ann left the room with everyone talking and asking questions.

"What is she talking about?" Craig asked Doug.

"I really don't know," said Doug. "We spent hundreds of hours in the lab perfecting the creation formula. This, as far as I am concerned came from us and our research."

The group left the room after more discussion and decided to just continue on with what they had set out to do.

Chapter Thirteen: Unparalleled

The building of the second and larger ship had taken its toll on everyone and a few days of rest and relaxation were called for. The construction was almost complete, but this would give everyone a chance to unwind.

They planned a barbeque and a relaxed mood was in the air. A couple of cows were slaughtered for the event. Basketball and football games were played by the large group of people that now occupied the old airstrip. People were still needed to stand guard in the tower and a reaction team would rotate out too. They had been attacked only once in almost a year, but no one was about to let their guard down.

Jake went to see Samantha in her new quarters. After she had been released from the medical center, she wouldn't leave her room. Jake knocked on her open door and got no response, so he walked in.

"What can I do for you?" asked Samantha.

"My name is Jake and..."

"I know who you are," interrupted Samantha. "What do you want?"

"I wanted to see how you were doing and see if you needed anything," said Jake.

"I'm fine and no, now you can go," said Samantha.

Jake sat down at the foot of her bed and continued.

"I was shot in the head and was in a comatose state afterward," said Jake. "I woke up and could some-how remember everything just like I had been awake the whole time. What I'm trying to say is I can help you come to terms with your new gifts."

"I have a pretty good idea of what I can do now," said Samantha, "and I don't need a baby sitter. I will, however, take some comfort from you."

Samantha sat on Jake's lap and kissed him with a passion that took him by surprise. Jake stopped her. "Not that I don't want to, but don't you think we should get to know each other first?"

Samantha answered his question with more kiss-ing. She got up to close and lock the door. She then jumped on Jake and started to take his clothes off.

Up above at the entrance of the hangar, the barbeque was in full swing. The fresh vegetables and cooked beef that everyone continually thanked Simon, Susan and Nancy for were laid out on tables. The kids were in line first, then women and men. Everyone, even the newest people, were glad to be there. It was almost as if the bombs had never fallen, as they all enjoyed the festivities. Steve, James, Doug and Chris were at the front of the area of tables with their families and after everyone sat down with their food, Steve asked them all to calm down.

He then addressed the crowd.

"I want to thank everyone for their tireless efforts in all aspects of our community. We have all come light years from where we started just a few short years ago. Some of you have been with us from the beginning, and some of you have found your way to us. You all are part of the next step in our evolution as a species and we will rebuild this civilization."

Everyone was cheering and the hangar quickly got loud again as everyone continued to talk and eat. The night went great and a few of the people brought out musical instruments. After the dinner clean up, they all enjoyed the music and many people danced. There would be one more day of relaxation before getting back to work on the ship completion.

Jake and Samantha had come upstairs just as everyone was finishing dinner and were able to eat before the food was put away.

"Where've you been?" asked Joe as Jake walked by.

"We were talking," said Jake with a smile.

The guards in the tower were relieved by other men once they were done eating. No one wanted to miss the festivities, but the security of the compound was paramount and they all knew and accepted this.

After the R and R, the workers all assembled in the hangar to hear Doug outline what the plan was.

"We will be finishing this ship in a couple of weeks," said Doug. "I would like the fabricator crews to start on construction of the next ship while the final

160

steps are added to the Intrepidus. This is the name of the ship we are finishing now."

"What does it mean?" asked a man in the crowd.

"The name is Latin for fearless," said Doug.

The men cheered and went to their work areas.

"How many suits do you have done?" Doug asked Steve.

"We've completed five now," said Steve. "We'll need to fit everyone else as they become available. They're custom fit for the user."

"Sounds good," said Doug. "I want everyone that has the twenty-fourth chromosome to have one."

"We'll need to get more material for that," said James as he walked into the conversation. "We'll let you know when we get low and need to go back out for more."

"Okay guys, great job," said Doug.

The ship was completed in ten days and it was ready to be taken out for its initial tests. Everyone gathered in front of the hangar and the new ship was brought out. This time it took all four Hummers to tow it onto the airstrip. The ship was twice the size of the first one and would aid greatly in the gathering of raw materials for the next five that would be built. Doug had told everyone that as more ships were built, they would be done faster each time.

The ship was put through its ground tests just like the Virtus had been. Jim was the pilot of this one. After all the systems checked out, Jim extended the legs and brought the ship to a rest on the airstrip. Steve gathered a dozen men and women that would get to experience the first flight of the first cruiser-class ship. The people all got on board and just like they had done with the Virtus, all of the maneuvering thrusters were tested with small bursts. A few hatches opened up and the weapons came out into view and then were retracted. Every control station reported everything nominal, so Jim took the ship up to a high hover. The ship and crew then flew off with great speed.

Jim took the Intrepidus through its paces and was happy with the results. He told everyone to get ready for weightlessness and pushed the engines to maximum velocity. The ship climbed with ease and was through the Karman line in just a few minutes. As they climbed, he let off the engine's acceleration while the atmosphere got thinner. They were soon through the thermosphere and he continued on through the exosphere. The ship was now more than four thousand miles above the earth. Jim was smiling as he turned around in his seat. The observation windows were opening so all on board could see where they were.

"How far are we away from the earth?" asked Steve.

"We're just over four thousand miles away," said Jim. "I'm very pleased with this vessel. We could be to the moon in a few hours and to Mars in a week if we wanted."

Jim turned back around in his seat and closed the viewing windows.

"Everyone stay in your seats," said Jim as he turned the ship around and headed back toward earth.

The trip back went by very fast and this time, they flew by the International Space Station. It was still in a good orbit according to Jim.

The ship was flown to a low orbit around the planet to survey and test the systems that had been added to this one. The viewing windows on the sides were opened back up for everyone to see the view of the earth from up close. Only a few people at a time could unbuckle and go look. It would be chaos if they all got out of their seats in the weightless environment without being used to it.

The long distance radar was picking up everything and putting it into the ship's computer in order of importance, from space junk to different sized meteorites to anything on the planet. The first voyage of the newest ship, Intrepidus had already proven to be productive. A massive fleet of battleships, submarines and aircraft carriers had been spotted in the vastness of the Pacific Ocean. They appeared to be coming from the Asian region of the Pacific and heading east toward what was left of the United States. This was the first larger ship that had been completed and should be able to handle the fleet if needed, but as Jim, Chris and Steve discussed everything they decided that if they engaged the fleet, they should bring the scout ship in as well. With the reflective shielding, both ships would be no match for the conventional firepower of the advancing force. It was unclear what the fleet's intentions were, but they were headed from the area that launched the first nuclear bombs as far as they all knew, which started the beginning of the end. So this could be an invading force. Regardless of whom they were and why they were headed in the direction of the United States, they could end up being a threat to the people that lived on the airstrip and had to be intercepted to find out for sure. Pictures and video were taken of the fleet from orbit to get a better idea of what the advanced ships might be facing.

The ship broke orbit and made its way through the upper atmosphere and continued on with no problems as the engines slowed its descent. The design worked perfectly. Normally any object that would enter into the gravitational pull of a planet would enter with such great velocity that it could burn up. That's why the ceramic shielding was used on space shuttles. They had no way of slowing their decent like the new ship did. Jim flew the ship down through thirty thousand feet above the old East Coast. The observation windows had all been opened up again so that everyone onboard could get a closer look at the ground and they headed south toward their airstrip. As they all got out of their seats to look, the destruction that everyone saw was unimaginable.

The Intrepidus was on its way toward Idaho and their airstrip. The fleet of ships heading for the old West coast had to be an occupation force and it would not be good if they made it to shore. The decision to go out and meet them would have to be discussed as a group.

The ship flew around the city before landing over by the main hangar. Many people on the ground could be seen looking up. Once they landed, Jim powered down and lowered the ramp. Doug went aboard to see how everything went. Everyone was getting off and Jim was still sitting at the flight controls making sure that everything looked good.

"How did she do?" asked Doug.

"This is an amazing ship," said Jim. "We need to get the group together."

Jim handed Doug some of the pictures of the fleet heading for the coast.

"I agree," said Doug.

They left the ship and headed inside to round everyone up. Steve was already starting to find people and asking them to go to the meeting area in the basement.

Within half an hour, the whole group had assembled to discuss the incoming threat. Jim handed the pictures out and they were passed around.

"We don't know who they are or why they are coming," said Jim. "As you can see, the fleet is massive and would pose a grave threat to our near future. The lives of everyone around us are a good enough reason to go out there and find out what they are doing, and the ongoing construction of our ships is secondary."

"We should at least go out there and try to talk to them," said Doug.

They were all in agreement and started to plan for a possible attack on the compound as well. Doug and Jim would pilot the two ships. A small strike force along with a few suit soldiers would accompany each ship. The next day they would prepare the ships and everyone going.

"I'm scared," Karen told Steve that night.

"It will all be okay honey," said Steve. "Do you remember how scared you were when I went out to test the suit?"

"Yes," said Karen, "but this is different."

"Not at all," said Steve. "The technology we have is way beyond anything else out there. We will be unstoppable, and that's one of the reasons that we need to be careful where the gene therapy is concerned. If it got into the wrong hands, they could destroy the planet or the universe for that matter. You will understand better once you have been inoculated."

Karen, Steve and De Novo went to sleep. The next day would be another long one.

The hangars and the surrounding area of the airstrip were quiet all night long. Early the next morning, Doug was already running diagnostics on the Virtus. Jim was out not long after doing the same with the Intrepidus. Jake and Joe were the first ones in the armory that morning getting their gear prepped. The whole main hangar was awake before long and they all went about their duties. After the introduction of all the new people, it worked better to just have certain people do one job other than rotating. Some people would swap out from time to time in order to be more proficient or to take a break from the monotony.

After breakfast, the day's work started. Some areas would be shorthanded due to some people leaving to check out the incoming fleet.

Construction of the next ship would continue with Jill in charge of the fabrication. She was the next pilot to take charge of a new ship and was still considering its name.

Ann would take command of one of the new ships too, once she had her baby.

The strike teams and suit soldiers assembled in front of the hangar and Craig looked them all over. Coms were checked and the men and women walked up the ramps of their designated ships. The occupants of the airstrip all stopped what they were doing to watch them take off.

The two ships rose side-by-side and slowly headed south toward the ocean. They both rose to thirty thousand feet and started scanning the area with their radar. Another ship was detected heading toward the fleet out in the ocean, so the Intrepidus shot up to a higher altitude to get a look at it. With the magnification on the cameras, the men could see that the ship was flying the United States flag.

"Is she protecting the U.S. all by herself?" asked Joe.

"Not if I can help it," said Jim. "Virtus, this is the Intrepidus, we need to show the American aircraft carrier that we're friendly. Can you do that please?"

"Roger that Intrepidus," said Doug.

The USS Carl Vinson was a Nimitz class super carrier based out of San Diego California before the war. It was the flagship of a carrier strike group, but it was the only ship that they could pick up in the area. The ship's call sign was "Gold Eagle."

Doug took the ship in low and fast above the ocean to try and avoid their radar. He planned to come up alongside the ship and communicate via his radio.

As the ship approached the carrier, a Sea Wiz cannon fired on the Virtus. Doug wasted no time and tried to contact the captain as the bullets were deflected.

"USS Carl Vinson, this is the earth ship Virtus. We mean you no harm and wish to talk to your captain," said Doug.

The automatic cannon stopped firing.

"This is Captain Nathan Scott, say again your last. You are an earth ship? Are you American or not?"

"Captain, we don't have much time until the approaching fleet is within strike distance," said Doug. "We want to assist you, but we need to talk. Can we land on your flight deck?"

There was no response for a few minutes as the ship flew beside the carrier and then the radio came alive.

"Earth ship Virtus, you have permission to land on the forward flight deck. Do you need any assistance?"

"Gold Eagle, this is Virtus, negative on assistance. We are on our way," said Doug.

Doug took the ship up and hovered above the flight deck. He extended the legs and landed.

"Virtus, you are to power down your engines and prepare to be boarded," said a sailor on the radio.

"Again I tell you that we mean you no harm," said Doug. "Your auto cannon had no effect on this ship and neither will any other weapons you have in your arsenal.

We will lower our ramp and accept a small, unarmed delegation. The ball is in your court," said Doug.

The ramp of the Virtus was lowered. Steve and Jake walked out in suits to stand on either side of the ramp.

Marines took positions on both sides of the control tower and six men started walking toward the ship.

"What the hell is going on here?" the commander of the air group asked the chief while watching from the control tower.

"I have no idea sir," said the chief. "Earth ship they said? Our weapons had no effect on them and they were only fifty feet away. What kind of technology do they have?"

"Hopefully they're on our side," said the CAG. "I didn't have much hope in surviving the engagement we were about to undertake."

The captain and his detail approached the Virtus. As they got close, one of the Marines moved to the side and brought something up with his hand. Steve's cannon came out of his arm and Jake did the same as he opened his shield. The detail stopped and the Marine dropped his camera. Steve and Jake put their weapons away and motioned for the men to board. They followed the captain and his men onto the ship. The ramp stayed down as they boarded.

Doug met them in the cargo bay. He saluted the captain and said, "I'm Commander Doug..."

"Stockton," finished the Captain. "I recognize you. You went up with the last shuttle to the space station just days before the bombs fell," said Scott, "but you were older I thought."

"Yes sir, I am that Doug Stockton," said Doug.

"You need to tell me what the hell is going on here son," said Scott.

"It's a very long story sir and we don't have time to go over it. This ship is very advanced and that is all I can tell you right now. We have a sister ship that will join us if you want our help," said Doug. "Here's the radio if you can tell your men to stand down while she enters weapons range."

"What are these?" The captain pointed at Steve and Jake.

"Those are suits that we also developed," said Doug. "I know this is a lot to take in at once sir, but if you trust that what I am telling you is real then we need to act now. I will tell you everything else once the threat coming at us is neutralized," said Doug.

The captain looked around at everyone and got on the radio.

"XO, this is the captain. Another ship is going to appear in front of the carrier and you are to do nothing. I'm going up with them to engage the incoming fleet if they attack. I want you to launch all fighter aircraft and maintain a two hundred mile ready line once we are airborne."

"Roger that captain," said the XO with tension in his voice.

The Intrepidus flew into view and the captain looked at Doug.

"That one is bigger," said the captain.

"Yes sir," said Doug. "The one we are on is just a scout ship, fighter class. The one in front of you is a cruiser class ship called the Intrepidus."

"You're giving all of your ships Latin names," said Scott with a smile. "Let's see what these babies can do."

Doug offered the seat next to him to Captain Scott and started flipping switches and pushing buttons. He grabbed a joystick in front of him. The ramp went up and the ship took off to join the Intrepidus. The other men that came on board with the captain were asked to take seats at the back of the bridge. The two ships were flying side by side as they approached the massive fleet.

"I thought Bruce Lindsey was the captain of the Carl Vinson?" Craig asked Scott.

"He was, but when the call to action came down, the battle group was at anchor while we were getting ready to re-deploy," said Captain Scott.

"Many of our men were on shore leave," said a Marine.

"That's right, they didn't all make it back in time before we were ordered to get underway and hunt the submarines that attacked the United States," said Scott. "Captain Lindsey was one of them."

"Central command appointed the next senior officer in succession to command the battle group before the radio went silent, which happened to be me," said Scott.

"Ours was the only ship that has survived the last two years that we know of, and with a skeleton crew," said the Marine with rank insignias of Master Sergeant.

"So, why were you going to take on such a large force?" asked Craig.

"We are the last line of defense that the West Coast has and we will die defending it," said Scott.

"We sent up an AWACS to monitor the incoming fleet two days ago. It was shot down along with its two escorts. These people aren't messing around," said the captain. "They sent up thirty more jets before I could even scramble an alert."

"Do you know who they are?" asked Doug. "We couldn't see any flags, but they look like a mix of Russian and Chinese style ships."

"You know more than me," said the captain. "They haven't responded to our radio calls and we've been trying for over a week to contact them."

"This is one of the orbital pictures that we took last week," said Chris.

"Thank you," said the captain as he took the photo from Chris. "You have the latest of everything don't you?" asked the captain. "What satellite took this clear of a picture?"

"We didn't use any satellites," said Doug. "The Intrepidus took that on her maiden voyage the other day, from orbit."

The captain had a look of disbelief on his face.

"Like I said, it's a long story," said Doug. "We're approaching two hundred miles, everyone to battle stations. Everyone else, take a seat and buckle up."

Jim was piloting the Intrepidus and tried to contact the fleet, but got no response. "They must be completely encrypted," he said. "Either that, or they don't want to talk. I can't pick up any radio traffic coming from them."

The viewing window in front of the flight deck was covered with the skin of the ship and a HUD came into view.

"Incredible," said the captain, as all of the ships, aircraft and submarines came into view on the display. They could all be seen in real time. They could see that more aircraft were being launched and the ships were getting into a battle formation.

The two ships stopped and hovered while they continued to try to contact the fleet.

"We have six incoming," Jim told Doug over the radio.

"I see them."

"Are you going to fire on them? This ship does have weapons right?" asked Captain Scott.

"We will only engage them if they fire first," said Doug. "They want to see what we are and they might get close enough for us to see them too, and yes we have weapons."

"I saw only a shell of a ship," said the captain. "What kind of weapons do you have?"

"Craig can you show the captain our complement please?" asked Doug as he pointed toward Craig.

"Over here sir," said Craig.

The captain got out of his chair and walked over to another console.

"Here are our ion pulse cannons," said Craig as he pointed them out on a display of the ship.

"Ion pulse cannons?" said the Captain.

"Yes," said Craig. "They are basically very advanced rail guns. The men in the suits have small versions of them too."

Jake opened his right forearm up and his cannon came out and then went back in. "They also have the same repulsion technology that the ships do. All bullets and missiles will just be pushed away," said Craig.

"You might want to take your seat captain," said Doug, "they're getting close."

The jets flew by and rolled away. The cameras onboard were taking pictures as they approached and got some good ones.

"They have North Korean markings on them," said Craig as he sent over a picture to the HUD for Doug and Captain Scott to see.

"They're coming back," said Jim.

This time the jets fired missiles at the ships. They of course had no effect and the ships opened fire with the ion cannons, destroying them.

Jim tried again to contact the fleet and again got no response. Anti-aircraft flak started to explode all around them as they got closer to the fleet, and they could see that a huge attack force of jets was inbound. The flak was pushing them around the sky with each burst. It was all being deflected, but the shock waves from the explosions hit them and made it a little more difficult to fly.

"Let's take care of these jets and then deal with the ships," Doug said to Jim.

"We're right beside you," said Jim. "I guess you could say that diplomacy has failed."

The two ships flew in to intercept and engage the incoming jets as the barrage of anti-aircraft flak continued to push them around.

The scene of the firefight in the sky must be spectacular from down below, thought Craig, as he continued to blow jets out of the sky with the ion pulse cannons.

"We have more inbound," Doug said to Jim.

"Let's go get 'em boys!" yelled Craig enthusiastically.

About The Author

Travis Wright was born and raised in a small, Oregon town, where his love of the outdoors first began. He grew up hunting and fishing in the rural northwest, a lifestyle that transferred easily to a life in the last frontier. Wright has been in Alaska for 22 years, and now lives in Soldotna with his wife and five children – a daughter and four teenage boys.

When he's not busy with his family or trekking through backcountry, Wright works in the retail gun store he's owned and operated for 14 years. He is an NRA certified instructor and enjoys teaching others gun skill and safety.

Wright's interest in firearm technology as well as his active duty in the Marine Corps infantry are both influential in his work as a writer. While Wright has written poetry off and on for most of his adult life, his work as a novelist began in 2010 with the survival story Uncertain Times. Since putting that work to rest, he hasn't stopped writing. Wright's lifelong active imagination and curiosity have found their outlet in storytelling.

More ideas for stories are emerging all the time. Look for them to be published soon.